Timothie Hill and the Cloak of Power

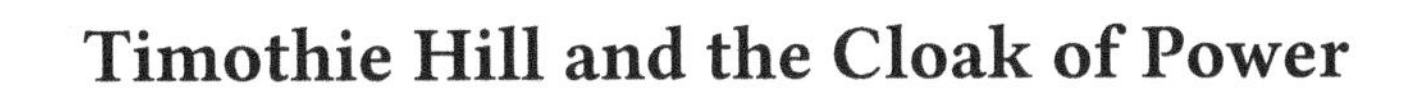

Timothie Hill and the Cloak of Power

Kenna Mary McKinnon

Published 2018 by Creativia
Cover art by Cover Mint

Chapter One

"Wow, Timothie, I love the purple spikes." The older woman perched on a silver chair while her stylist twirled his hands through her lavender hair. She settled the salon's cape around her shoulders.

"Why don't you try this, luv?" he asked and spun on one shiny black boot, the silver buckles sparkling in the sun that poured like honey through the spacious windows of his salon. "I can put you under the dryer, and the color will last longer. Then style your hair like this and this – that's right. Come with me. Magazine? Coffee? Is the music too loud for you?"

"You promise you'll make me look young again?" The woman pulled at her left earlobe and smiled. She strode to the dryer and settled herself under the hood. Timothie brought her black coffee. The roar of the dryer drowned out the sound of Jann Arden singing "Under June."

* * *

In the district of Oliver, across the city, Timothie's old friend and nemesis hunched over a pentagram carved into the floor tiles of his condo penthouse. Something sloshed in the basin by his elbow. New York, where he'd last worked in advertising, was a checkered memory. Only Edmonton was real; the gateway to Hell.

Reginald Smith chuckled. New York hadn't worked out. They'd hated him there, like the company he worked for in Edmonton hated him until he'd promised to make them billions with an invention from the dark side. TopStrategy Marketing didn't know they were dealing with the dark side. They didn't care to know.

Thick clots of blood and smoke combined to choke the stocky blond man, who peered into the eyes of the summoned apparition. Bael, the head of sixty-six legions of demons in Hell, desultorily granted supernatural powers to his minions on Earth. Reginald's lip curled below his blond mustache. He seldom made use of invisibility. Surely, there were other, more potent, superpowers denied to him.

He poured the holy water into the middle of the pentagram. Bael roared and flowed clockwise down the drain set into the blue tiles and the symbols that had summoned him. It was not yet the demon's time to make his presence known to Earth. Reginald would help it with that awful task when the time came. This was only a trial run for the man and the demon, and Reginald made sure he was in control. He feared the power of the demon but was excited, as well.

* * *

Timothie threw the black cloak with the silver stars across his bulging biceps. A blast of cold air buffeted the glass doors and rattled the sign in front of his salon.

Maude slipped out the side door, knowing more than she ought to know in this moment of his transformation.

"Turn off the lights," she called as she strode to her 1979 Mercedes Benz parked at the curb. Smoke coughed from the exhaust as the engine roared to life. She and her vintage automobile vanished from Timothie's sight as they rumbled beneath the Old Towne of Beverley sign and west on 118 Avenue.

"'Bye, Maude," the hairstylist whispered. Since his assistants, Skye and Paula, had gone home, the salon now sat in darkness. As he glided outside, the wind whipped Timothie's lithe form to an angle reminiscent of the superhero he really was. His cloak billowed over his broad shoulders. He rose into the air. All dust, wind, and fury, the Angel of the West flashed by, and Timothie was held in her arms, invisible, and hurled to the pinnacle of the tallest building in this city of champions. In a spacious room at the top of the towering apartment spire, he confronted his old friend, Reginald, who cowered as the dark froth that had been Bael swirled down the drain to the nether regions.

"What is this?" Reginald asked and held out his arms. "Timothie, you must be a ghost."

Reginald intermittently still clung to Timothie and the hairstylist's goodness. Timothie's superpowers were a surprise when he unveiled the Cloak of Power that allowed him to fly and granted invisibility. His friend's secret weapon, the Cloak, was alarming to Reginald, whose own secrets were darker and far more dangerous.

Timothie's baritone voice soothed the hunched figure who sprinkled holy water across the cursed blue tiles of his penthouse floor. "I'm the spirit of Draxxt, not to harm a soul on this enchanted planet, Earth."

"Draxxt, that planet you say you're from? You're a hairstylist from Vancouver. You don't seem to have a family. Maybe you *are* a ghost; a disembodied spirit who can fly through walls. I know you, old friend. You can't fool me. I haven't seen you for months. Now you just appear here, and I must have left the door open, because I don't believe in aliens who can fly through walls, and I don't believe in ghosts. You're not welcome. Get the frig out, little bastard."

"I was born with two good parents. Both were killed in the Troll Wars. The king was like a father to me. You choose not to believe that I'm the favorite of kings. Now there's something bigger than both of us that needs our attention, because you're smack in the middle of something dreadful."

"You didn't grow quickly; you grew crazy, dude. What's this about Trolls?" In the background, a small TV droned on about the President of the United States, Dennis Ducksworth, and his policy against globalization. Somehow the news of the day seemed to fit their conversation.

"The magic of the Trolls threw me back to Earth, darling. You know that, and I think you're afraid. I'm a superhero on Earth, Reginald. You never believed that part of me. It's only now coming out, the magic, the blessing, the Angel from God."

Reginald rubbed his eyes. "I don't know you as Superman," he said. "I know you as an old friend. I think you spout nonsense, dude. You aren't from another planet, though I've often thought you were! If anything..." The hunched man placed the basin by his feet and stood. "...if anything, Tim, you're a fool. I knew that all along when I was abusing you, when you left our relationship, and now that you've come back like this, when I don't need you anymore, I think you *could* be an angel. Marriage was too easy here in Canada. It didn't work out. You see now what I am?"

Timothie frowned. "Yes, and it doesn't change anything between us, anything we thought we knew about each other. Both of us are spiritual in our own way."

A faint whiff of sulfur curled among the beams above his head. "Though spiritual can be a two-edged sword, my old friend. You chose the dark side, and Draxxt be damned."

His friend snorted. "You're wrong, darling. Everything's changed now that I've reached my maturity." He pushed his glasses further up the bridge of his nose. "Now, we have a demon to engage, I think, and soon, too."

"No!" cried Timothie. "Don't interfere with my powers!"

"That's my destiny."

Timothie chewed on his lower lip. "I'm a force of good in a universe of evil."

Reginald smoothed his fair short-cropped hair. "I'm not evil. Bael is evil. He's my servant. He does what I tell him now that I have my mother's old book of spells, and I use him for good purposes. He has power, and I have the destiny. Now get out of our friggin' way."

"Impossible. You don't use evil for good purposes. He's twisted your brain, Reg. I'm here to help you overcome what could be the biggest mistake of anyone's life – getting involved with the dark force."

"Not all bad," Reginald said, his hazel eyes glinting with an unholy light. "It's pleasure, Timothie, not pain. The dark force uses pleasure to get through this unholy life that God has given us."

The penthouse seemed to sway with the force of the gale outside that pounded the glass windows and whipped blinding sleet against their reflections in the pane. Timothie's black, star-speckled cape swung about his manly shoulders as he levitated three feet above the floor. Invisible to anyone else, the Angel of the West embraced the stylist with the salt and pepper hair, the dark eyes, and the stubbled chin, and loved him with tender eyes.

"I love you, too," murmured Timothie to the Angel. They joined hands and disappeared through the wall of the apartment.

Reginald was sure this apparition of his old friend and the heavenly host had something to do with the demon Bael whom he had summoned a short time ago. He glanced at the wall clock. Three o'clock in the morning! The tiles were dry, the basin emptied, and Bael gone.

"I'm not evil," Reginald objected.

"You're just drawn that way, like Jessica Rabbit." A deep hollow voice guffawed from the corners of the room – whether the voice originated with Bael, Timothie, or the Angel of the West, Reginald was uncertain. The cream-colored walls of his entertainment room erupted with filthy cartoon pictures, caricatures of famous presidents and premiers, he and his former partners posturing obscenely across the expanse of wall to the gold Venetian blinds where the black sleet pounded on the windows. There was Nancy and John, Little Jim, Brandi, Maryjane, Klein, rabbits and Elmer Fudd, the fat boy in the striped shirt with a hard-on for Lucy, and his mother and father! His friends and family, and there – *there* was a young Reginald, doing what he did behind closed doors coming out of the closet where he had melted the hangers and hinges. There was his first piano teacher he called Mr. Roboto, and then – marching across the walls in a riot of black and white, the pictures changed to neon colors and slithered out the window into the night where, Reginald was sure, the entire world would learn of his infidelities and the obscene drama of his life.

* * *

Timothie, secure in the arms of the Angel, plummeted down to Ada Boulevard where he lived in a condominium with a southern river view fronting a quaint old Victorian mansion. Wrapped in his cloak, the stylist's limbs and body remained warm and dry. Suddenly, he was home. Timothie's bedroom sparkled with fairy lights. A Himalayan salt lamp burned cozily like rock candy. He pulled back the crazy quilt on his double bed and spread the black velvet warmth of his cloak over it. What a day! He couldn't sleep.

True power did not come from a demon like Bael. The demon would grant power to those who spoke the correct incantations, but Reginald could not summon the entire coterie of attending sprites. His spells summoned only Bael, and Bael was limited when alone. Timothie's cloak, however, possessed abilities beyond anyone's imagination.

The Troll, Mindbender, provided the perfect opportunity to leave the security of Draxxt and engage in the magic which brought Timothie to Earth. He found the old magic and the old books. The blessed prayers taught to him by the great Troll would eventually summon an Angel to help him in his new life on this confusing Earth. Maude, a witch on Draxxt, came with him to assist.

The Angel of the West, alive in fire and kindling crimson eyes, warm arms, and powerful beating wings, offered a direct link to the existence of the God whom Timothie only recently comprehended. The cloak served as a bedcover at night, slipping him into restful dreams. It tendered protection and power during the day. It loaned invisibility when needed, the ability to fly beyond his dreams of flying, and the ability to see spirits. The cloak was his lover and friend, and he needed no other. Except, of course, for the Angel who had supplied it.

He knew that to an orphan and superhuman traveler such as he, magic had its price, and he may pay dearly for the privilege. Somewhere in the night, he knew, the Angel shielded his home with relentless huge and beating wings.

His protective Angel of the West. Timothie shuddered. "I love you, too," he whispered.

Chapter Two

Timothie threw the covers off his bare chest and leaped to the side of the room. There was no alarm clock. He didn't need one. He knew, though, that he had overslept. His salon business could not be neglected, and yesterday had been a day of adventure and plans following Maude's purple hair visit.

"Reginald!" he remembered. The universe cried out for redemption.

Timothie knew that Bael's appearance was only the first of many. Reginald, his old friend and nemesis, was an antihero wrapped in a cloak of invisibility and power provided by the demon. There was work to be done, not all of it as a super hairstylist, but some to be done that night back at the penthouse tower. The Angel had whispered in Timothie's ear earlier that week that all was not well at the Oyster nor with the world, and the Angel was always right. Timothie's mouth curved upward in a wry smile and his stubbled face smiled back at him in the sweat of the mirror.

After a quick power breakfast shake, shower, and shave, Timothie dressed in his black jeans, western belt, and tight white lace sleeveless shirt. He tucked his cloak into a gym bag, threw open the door to the adjoining carport, and vaulted into the seat of his red 1967 Volvo GT 123. The engine purred as he threw it into first gear and quickly accelerated into overdrive along Ada Boulevard. An instant later, the car sprouted silver wings and careened to the back of the salon and spa on 118 Avenue as though teleported, and perhaps it had, thought Timothie. He shoved the stick shift into "Park" and strode into the back of his salon.

The salon business was slow that morning, and Skye, the aesthetician from the backroom spa, melted into his arms to slow dance amongst the chairs, mirrors, and horse chestnut vines. Over the blare of the antique stereo, they conversed in short witticisms. Skye wore a smart black pantsuit and oxfords, her long auburn hair bobbed.

"I finished my advanced certificate exam this week," she explained as they twirled. "I can now do sugaring."

"Your certificate exams – what did you get on them?" Timothie asked. He pirouetted.

"Nail polish," Skye replied, and they both laughed.

"Dear," he said, "you look very like a man."

She peered at him with twinkling eyes and replied, "So do you."

He grinned his crooked smile, said, "You're beautiful," held her tightly, and they whirled to the door as a portly gentleman entered the narrow lobby.

Surprised, he beamed at them both as they broke apart. kd lang crooned "Bird on a Wire" from vinyl on the stereo. Skye skittered to the spa in the backroom, and the client settled into a silver chair. Timothie whisked his best apron around the gentleman's neck. Paula peered out from the waiting room.

"Dancing again?" she asked.

"Go, go," the stylist insisted, waving his hands. "I can't concentrate. You see I'm working." The client glanced up and grinned at the second aesthetician dressed in a purple smock and pink skirt.

"I've embarrassed you," Paula laughed.

Timothie examined his work, his client's greyish locks curling on the shiny hardwood floor. "You could never embarrass me. But go back to your spa, now. I can't concentrate when you're twittering."

"Ooo la la," Paula said and was joined by Skye, who took her by the arm and led her back amongst the mirrors and vines and brightly colored paintings to the rooms they rented for pedicures, manicures, and facials.

The gym bag shuddered in its place on the corner table by the spacious windows. The client tipped handsomely and left. Pages of a magazine fluttered. Paula came out and swept the floor. Timothie stood silhouetted at the window, the storm of last night dissipated into the fog of early morning, and an orange and lavender sunrise broke over the buildings to the east. He longed to don the cloak and be swept southwest to the spot where Bael's power was greatest, to confront the demon and its minion, and draw on the might of the Angel of the West. The tips of his sensitive fingers tingled. He felt cold.

With quick movements, he ransacked the gym bag, drew out the Cloak of Power, and threw it over his shoulders. The cloak swirled and covered his manly chest. The cloak was darker than a black Labrador, and the stars shone like silver holes seen through a velvet drape. Timothie's red shoes hovered six inches above the floorboards. He felt that rush of adrenaline that only the superhero can experience when his future explodes in his mind's eye – suddenly he knows that in the next instant he will be miles above his mundane neighbors and another adventure has begun.

No time for styling hair today, no time for Paula or Skye simpering in the backrooms, no time, no time! The door blew open with a thud, Jann Arden sang "Living Under June" on a vinyl LP, and Timothie was gone, transported into the orange-lavender burst of dawn, a twinkle of white soles, red shoes, a billowing cape, and the beat of the Angel's wings, no more but the grit of morning blowing about the Olde Towne of Beverley. He disappeared, teleported into Reginald's entertainment room in the district of Oliver, southwest, where the minion crouched by the flickering images on his wall and drooled in anticipation of another visit from Bael.

"Not you," Reginald whined. "It's the demon I summoned." The pentagram writhed in the middle of the room. Smoke, blood, and vomit poured from the basin Reginald held in his shaking hands.

"STOP!" Timothie roared, and extended a strong fist.

The apparition in the middle of the blue tiles hesitated then strengthened, erupting into a figure twelve feet high whose tentacles touched the beams on the high ceiling. Each black appendage sprouted a red eye with a white slit for the pupil.

The ultimate shapeshifter, Bael had usurped the throne of Hell from Lucifer and now set loose on Earth to imprison as many human souls as possible. He sought to strengthen the armies of Hell and, finally, become God in Heaven himself. All this Timothie knew from the whisperings of the Angel of the West. All this he knew from the Troll on Draxxt, the planet where he had grown as a youth and then been propelled to Earth by a burst of Mindbender's magic. Timothie knew his place in the universe – to vanquish the demon finally and lay peace to the nations of Earth.

Even Maude, the purple dream maker of spiked hair, didn't know the extent of his powers. She guessed because in her dotage she was wise. In a previous life, she had lived as a witch on Draxxt who sold the new queen a fertility charm to keep the pregnancy safe.

It worked, and Timothie remembered the queen and her husband, and of course, Tevron, the king's brother, and Tevron's wife. They raised him to a strapping adolescence. Then Mindbender took over Timothie's tutelage and instructed him in the art of magic. The Troll taught him his destiny on the world from which the humans of Draxxt had sprung so long ago. From Earth.

In Vancouver, he learned a trade, his skillful fingers deft and finally, practiced. The magic they held transferred to the flowing strands of his client's heads. Timothie was eager to learn, and the Angel of the West took him under her beating wings and her beating, loving heart. He learned well.

Now he confronted his nemesis, Bael, and his old friend Reginald, who had in his way taken the demon's form and power.

The black, white, and red image before him swayed in the putrid air of Reginald's room. Reginald drooled in his corner. The demon slobbered and groaned, tentacles in the place of its head. Timothie stood tall, hands on his slim hips, a silver sword suddenly at his side. He placed wiry but muscular fingers on the hilt of the sword, and drew it.

Bael lunged. Reginald lunged at the same time, a mirror image of Bael. Reginald's left hand gripped Timothie's right shoulder, the arm that held the sword. Through the dank, putrid air his hand blurred like silver fire, the sword slashed blue with sparks, and Reginald collapsed, screaming. Bael roared and fell on the caped figure, enveloping Timothie in blood and vomit. "You don't need me, superhero. Do it now!" The stylist could hear his Angel whisper. He rose above the clinging tentacles and the moans of the demon, rose to the cedar beams of his former friend's ceiling, and slashed at the writhing head.

The room was devoid of human sound. Only the echo of a demonic wailing and the roars of Hell below deafened the stylist. His sword glowed like a supernova a. Pierced by light, clouds scudded to the north. A south wind was always good, Timothie thought. Fog tendrils clawed at Reginald's windows. Designs of yellow and blue curled in intricate patterns on the floor.

Timothie slashed with the striking sword; sparks and lightning flew, a cacophony of sound rose, and Reginald gasped, "Enough!" He drew the basin of unholy fluids into his arms and emptied it onto the pentagram. He uttered the spell that would send Bael back to its kingdom beneath the ground.

Bael laughed.

Timothie groaned, and the sword catapulted from his hands. Fatigued, he collapsed to the floor. The cape with the silver stars covered his body. "My Angel, where are you?"

His spent words rasped into the silence. There was no reply.

Chapter Three

ZAP! Timothie's head reeled. His brains were scrambled. He staggered to his feet, Timothie the son of Jevil and Tara from Draxxt, the parents whose death in the Troll wars had orphaned him as a young lad in the badlands. Saving people, including himself, was what he'd been taught to do. For most of his life, he'd been forced to live in the shadows, never revealing his true powers. Now, faced with the cowering Reginald and the simmering drain on the floor, the superhero bent and grasped his sparkling sword. On the planet Draxxt he had been almost inconsequential, a mere orphaned boy, until the king's court and the great Troll Mindbender molded and formed his character and physique to be this, an Angel's favorite on an alien world.

Reginald grinned in the corner. There was something odd about his appearance. Timothie swirled his Cloak of Power around his shoulders, the tight white lace of his shirt rippling across his chest.

"It almost had you there, Tim," Reginald said. "If I hadn't sent it back where it came from, you'd be a grub on the far wall."

"I owe you, Reg," agreed Timothie. "We go back a long way. Maybe I had you wrong."

His former friend cracked his knuckles. "Clever."

"I've never known you to crack your knuckles."

Reginald's face wavered. "Trying to butter me up, Tim? Think you can get a hold of the dark side that way? Win your fight without your precious Angel?" He cracked his knuckles again.

"My old friend never cracked his knuckles. Bael, the shapeshifter, doesn't have a policy against using his friends for professional reasons. Where is Reginald?" Timothie strode across the room in two strides, gripping the shuddering creature by his throat. Reginald's face dropped into gaping, bloody fangs and a core of putrid smell. It was Bael, the master shapeshifter, and the human lay inert, as though asleep, on the other side of the room.

"It is you!" Timothie cried and threw the demon against a wall of scrolling obscenities. "What have you done to my former friend? Is he dead, you monster? I swear I'll send you back to Hell, and you'll stay there!"

"HUMAN," Bael roared and dissolved into a pool of thick black fluid surrounded by crimson eyes. Only white slits in the eye sockets showed Timothie the demon's soft spots. The stylist planted his feet into the mire. Forks of lightning flashed from the mirrored panes of the windows. He hovered above the swirling fluid and the white slits that glared and sparked; the crimson eyes pulsed below his red shoes as he levitated six feet from the floor tiles.

"You're stronger than I thought," Timothie said. "Let's talk." He drew his sword and plunged it into the midst of the froth. He grinned his crooked smile and rubbed the stubble on his chin. Translucent in the ambient lighting, his close-cropped salt and pepper hair sparkled like the blade. Slouched in a corner, the real Reginald roused himself and watched.

"I have a spell. I won't use it, though," his human friend offered, lifting a limp hand in greeting.

Timothie's sword slurped as he pulled it from the mess on the floor. He catapulted to the ceiling and spread his sinewy arms. "I have a spell, too."

The demon heaved. Reginald pounded his fists on the wall of crude caricatures. "You're no match for his magic, Tim."

"Magic," Timothie said. "I learned it on my world."

"Your world? You mean Vancouver?" Reginald, his former friend and nemesis, rubbed his eyes and waved his arms in a circular pattern.

"You're a simple hairstylist from Vancouver. You learned your trade at Marvel Beauty Schools. I know you. You are nothing. Get him, Bael!"

"If spirits threaten me in this place, Fight Water by Water and Fire by Fire, banish their souls into nothingness, and remove their powers until the last trace. Let these evil beings flee, through Time and Space."

Huge snowy wings beat-beat. The Angel of the West spread her arms around Timothie, the black, star-spangled cloak secure on the stylist's shoulders. A river of scalding water cascaded from the vaulted ceiling and washed the demon toward the center of the blue tiles. Bael screamed and slithered down the drain. Timothie bellowed another incantation. "It's fine, Uriel. Thank you, my Defender of the Element of Water and of the West."

Bael in the form of Reginald was gone. The real Reginald adjusted his glasses, stood, and lit a joint. Outside, grey spires struck through the morning fog. Traffic crawled below. All seemed like a normal day in downtown Edmonton.

Timothie's mobile phone played "Dixie." The small blue instrument squawked. "Cut and color at one thirty tomorrow? Just a minute, let's see. Okay, can you make it for three? I'm down for that."

A normal day for superhero Timothie Hill.

Something obscene swirled on the edges of the blue tiles. It would be back.

Chapter Four

Initially, the next day at the salon proved interesting. Timothie swirled into the backroom, through Paula's waiting room, past Skye putting on her makeup, and grabbed a quick coffee before he entered the front rooms as hairstylist extraordinaire. His Ralph Lauren military brown belt with silver buckle coordinated perfectly with an Alexander McQueen white peasant boy lace shirt with brown French military boots and matching silver buckles. Black lambskin low-rise jeans completed the outfit. He tossed his gym bag onto the table by the ceramic pot of blooming impatiens. He imagined the Cloak of Power stirring inside the bag.

Now, his coffee cup to his lips, Timothie waited for his first appointment of the morning, a 30-something woman who worked in graphic design at Sapphire Designs on Alberta Avenue. She asked him to use his "special powers" to create a stunning hairdo that would knock them out at the annual meeting that night of creative designers from all over North America, including those with the best and most innovative stylists.

Timothie was up to the challenge. Starr, his client, sauntered through the front doors, threw her foxy cape on a hanger, and plumped into a silver chair in front of the mounted wall mirror. She smiled and wriggled herself into the chair as he settled the salon's cape around her shoulders. "Do your worst, Timothie. Surprise me. But you remember, no stripping the color from the lovely auburn I already have."

"Rainbow hair?" he asked and swept his hands through her blunt shoulder-length cut. "Five or six weeks ago, we ordered these rainbow gradient hand-dyed hair extensions just for you, Starlight. They'll add a pop of rainbow color to your lovely crown. They're hand sewn, clip-in, and double-woven at the back. Your shoulder length hair is perfect for these psychedelic tresses. I'm so excited!" He began initially to clip in violet and shocking pink extensions – seven of them – then neon yellow, lime green, screaming purple, crimson, and silver. Starr moaned.

"They're gorgeous!" she cried. "Just right. The girls will be so jealous. I have the best hairstylist in the world."

"If only you knew," Timothie remarked cryptically. "I'm the best in many worlds." He chuckled and drew out another bright extension, carefully weaving it into Starr's natural hair. The whole process took more than an hour and cost in excess of four hundred dollars, but the end result was well worth it. His client agreed. She paid him generously for the fiery, Woodstock-era tresses that cascaded down her back and twisted in psychedelic colors over her shoulders.

"Perfect. Is Skye still doing sugaring?"

"Of course."

"Does she have any openings this morning? My chin… "

"Yes," he said and smoothed his hands over the snug black leather jeans that slung low on his hips. He drew water in a basin and washed his hands to above the wrists, pushing the French lace closer to his manly forearms. "Just a minute, I'll call her." His assistant appeared almost instantly at the door to her waiting room, by the horse chestnut vines and the limited edition stainless steel coffee Bodum, which had been purchased on holiday.

"Ooo la la," Skye exalted. "That's fabulous, Timothie!"

Starr grinned and swung her legs off the silver chair. "Can you sugar my face quickly, Skye? I need to be at the office in forty-five minutes. Tops." She clapped her hands.

Skye pirouetted on one cream-colored Valentino canvas espadrille. "No problem."

Paula poked her frizzy pink head around the corner. "I could do a quick manicure."

"No, thanks," Starr declined. "I so need a sugaring. By the best." She winked at Skye, who threw her hands into the air and beckoned for the client to follow her into the back salon. Paula grasped her hand as she pranced by.

"Ooo, nice nails. Who did them?"

"I did them myself. Do you like the designs?"

"Pretty blush pink gel polish with lime palm trees – why didn't I think of that for you last time you were in? I know how you love Maui."

Starr and the assistants swished into the back rooms, past the French press and the horse chestnut vines, with a toss of lurid tresses and shoes clacking on the hardwood floors until, muffled by carpet, they disappeared from Timothie's view. Very pleased with his morning's work, the stylist slouched in his silver chair. With deft fingers, he dialed the bistro west of the Beverly sign. He ordered a gyro and diet Pepsi for his lunch. Momentarily, his next client would arrive. He would have time to eat and drink between afternoon appointments.

Timothie exhaled and studied his Android phone, the many icons blinking in psychedelic colors. Several calls had come in while he had been working on Starr's hair extensions. He began to call them back but was interrupted when his next client clacked through the front doors, throwing her light summer stole onto the hangers in front and settling herself in the chair Timothie had just vacated.

"Cut and color?" he asked, weaving his slim fingers through her black hair.

"Something different," she entreated. "How about something wild this time, my friend? The grey roots are beginning to show. I'm tired of matt black. Maybe something more youthful?"

Timothie clapped his hands. He laughed. He did enjoy a challenge. "I have just the thing."

"Gold highlighting?" he suggested. "Or should we try ash blonde?"

"I think that would be glorious," his client replied. "Oh, is that your lunch I see coming in the door? A deliveryman is lurking outside, and his little truck says, 'Italian Bakery.' I didn't know they were open again."

"Oh, yes, no problem," said Timothie as he smoothed the metal comb through her long, shining hair. "Just put it down there, dearie." He tipped the man and left the sandwich and soda on the table by the window. "I hope you don't mind, luv?"

"Oh, no," she said. "Not at all. A man's got to eat. Especially a superhero."

Timothie stopped mid-stride. "What?"

She laughed. "I think you're a super stylist. A real hero. As far as I'm concerned, anyhow."

"Oh." He laughed and levitated six inches off the floor. She didn't notice. He knew she wouldn't. He had power over minds like that – they didn't notice his peculiarities, or if they did, they loved him for them. Not unusual to levitate off the floor, he thought and smiled to himself, his handsome stubbled face thoughtful as he drew himself to the problem of how to make Mrs. Cardinal look young again.

Chapter Five

After his last client had gone home for the day, and Paula and Skye had closed their shop until tomorrow, Timothie the hairstylist slouched in his silver chair by the spacious windows of his salon, flicking through his phone messages, returning calls, and sipping coffee. The evening sun dipped low. The mobile glowed blue. Wait. Data streamed, hesitated – something was wrong. Timothie frowned. A notification appeared on Facebook, flickered, then disappeared. He'd had a momentary glimpse of a graphic of yellow roses. One notification. Disappeared. What is this caller trying to say? A friend inviting him to a party? Must know. Curiosity got the better of him.

He punched keys, trying to recover the name of the caller who planted anticipation in his mind. He was ready for a party or at least a coffee with an old friend. Life had been frenetic lately.

Timothie grinned. The mobile phone glowed. Yellow roses? He had an idea. As a gardener, he shared his passion with only one other friend.

Dark-skinned Crazy Jack Dareboy, he knew it in his bones. The other Draxxian. Or Minth, as the fairies would say. The humans had named the alien planet Draxxt, but the Fairy Queen saw humans as a temporary race and called the planet Minth from the very beginning when the fairies still existed in their domain tucked away beyond the sea. Now the magical Crazy Jack Dareboy was on Earth. Timothie grinned his crooked smile. Crazy Jack was third in heir to the throne of Gracklen, but had fled due to a family feud. He might be crazy, but he had royal blood.

The humans had fled to Draxxt too long ago to count as newcomers, Timothie thought, scratching his ribs. Now he and Dareboy were the newcomers on the Earth from which they'd sprung.

His memories were intact, more so because of the peculiar circumstances of his arrival on Earth from Draxxt. He arrived in a blast of smoke and fire, encased in the magic metal dragon like a roast in an oven. The rocket which first brought humans to Draxxt was rediscovered by Mindbender and the Picts, and furbished with magic and science. Crazy Jack had followed him, on magic and invisible forces, from the woodlands of the Picts and Trolls where he had been banished. Dareboy, muscular and svelte, with his wild black frizzy dreadlocks and the insane smile, a disappointment to his royal parents.

Timothie sat in the silver chair and cursed the mobile phone. He grinned and swore at his Facebook image. He snapped the off button on the phone. "Get up," he muttered to no one in particular. "Get up and find this guy."

"Lord give me patience."

His lambskin jeans smelled like new leather and creaked like a saddle as he strode to the windows, bootheels clacking on the hardwood floor. Smoke curled from his mobile, and he suspected that the boy was responsible, Dareboy, who had taken his place with Reginald two years after Vancouver.

From the face of his phone sputtered sparks and magical symbols. He knew there was only one entity besides Bael that could do that to an electronic device, and it wasn't Bael. Bael had his own modus operandi, and this wasn't it. Someone or something dark and humorous had followed him from Draxxt, perhaps as a gift from the universe, as he missed his old friends so much.

"Science and magic brought you here, Crazy Jack Dareboy," he muttered, "but, by Pete, I wanted to see my friends from Gracklen. They must have sent reinforcement with you to contain you, Crazy Dareboy. They're the ones I really want to see. Tevron, Mariette, my boys from the orphanage." He sighed, remembering his idyllic youth. Then how it all turned sour, after the new regime settled in with promises of peace and hope. The sourness of disillusionment.

Timothie muttered, "Dareboy is the boy who would be king on Draxxt." Dareboy was the Dracaena's cousin and nephew of Queen Almere and King Stannock. Nephew of King Tevron, who co-ruled with his brother, Stannock, after the death of the mad old King Hakor. The intrigue on Draxxt never stopped. Timothie had tired of it and migrated to the old planet, Earth, to escape its dangers, but he found here no escape from the same melodrama.

Crazy Jack Dareboy held his place as third in line to the throne of Draxxt, exiled by his black father because the boy was as mad as his grandfather, Hakor, and as vicious.

"You kept low, too, as I did." Timothie ripped open his gym bag and swung the Cloak of Power around his neck. Biceps bulged beneath his tight shirt.

He suspected that Dareboy was the inspiration behind his Facebook mystery message. He punched a number into the mobile. A text sprang up. "So, it's you, Timothie Hill! Reg told me you would be in touch. But I was first. Wasn't I?"

"First in nothing," he texted. Immediately his old friend responded.

"First in all things that matter. First in the Kingdom of Gracklen, of the planet of Draxxt. First in my cousin's esteem over his hybrid sister, the Dracaena. They call her Hope. Ha! Hope for nothing! He'll kill her there and take his rightful place on the throne of Gracklen. I'll help him, with the power I gather on Earth, which is ancient and meaningful on Gracklen of Draxxt."

"First you have to go through me," Timothie texted. "I'm the protector. I need to see the others you brought with you. My friends. From my own planet. The ones who accompanied you here to make sure you stayed."

"You must be so lonely." Timothie could feel the taunt through the glass of the mobile phone. The blue light dimmed.

"Meet me then. Without your cloak. You won't go far without your Angel to protect you."

Humans rediscovered science in those post-Hakor peaceful times on their adopted planet. Now Earth felt alien to them. But not to Timothie, who had in his brain the combined neuroplasticity of magic and science, fierce youth, and the will to overcome his innate anxiety, bequeathed to him by his parents before they died. They had left him with love before the arrows of the Troll Wars struck them down to Hades. His parents had instilled in him the intelligence that made it possible for Timothie to earn the Cloak of Power from Uriel, the Angel of the West.

Another text scrolled across the small screen, completing his thought. Crazy Boy was intermittently psychic. "Because only those with quirks above normal would properly understand the magic required to be what you became, my nemesis. Here on Earth. I hope you're happy here. You who would take our inheritance from us on Draxxt and who fled like a dog with his tail between his legs when things got too hot for you there. You were a simple gardener on Draxxt. That's all you'll ever be. Don't give yourself airs."

"I didn't come here to flee from you, Dareboy," he wrote. "I wanted friends and a new life. I don't owe you any friendship, and I don't forget that Reginald betrayed me for you."

"To me, you're the same gardener you always were, no superhero– your favorite plant, the horse chestnut vine, is even tattooed on your left bicep amongst crowns of roses and thorns. Gardening fool! Now you're a hair stylist, like Reginald was before he got dishonest. I would have done better than that choosing my friends, given your *interesting* lifestyle."

Timothie pictured in his mind the dark athletic form of Crazy Jack Dareboy. He slammed his thumbs into the keyboard. "I'm favored by God. I go with my cloak, given to me by the most powerful and gracious friend a human can possess. Did you take the young Reg away from me for spite? Is that what you're trying to say, darn you?"

"Suit yourself. Look out the window." The screen went dark.

Timothie shoved the phone into a tight-fitting rear pocket. Intermittent and muffled, traffic sputtered by on the avenue. Fluffy, cotton-soft cumulus clouds formed images over the city punctuated by a long white jet trail led by a silver dot, sliding through the heavens to the apex. Dropped below that scene – far below – a sturdy hooded figure in a burgundy and black jumpsuit crawled on the side of an opposing building.

It was Crazy Jack Dareboy, climbing the building to him. "Timothie."

"Where are the others?"

"I'm the only one left."

"You lie," Timothie whispered and beat his manly fists on the top of the table by the north windows. "You lie!"

He cried because he was so lonely for his old friends. Outside, Crazy Jack placed sucker-like palms on the glass panes and pressed his body into the salon. "That's all right," he said. "Jack's here."

Dareboy smiled. Timothie pressed his hands to the sides of his head and groaned. The Angel's wings beat-beat above the salon but seemed useless now. Timothie had not, after all, escaped the intrigues of Gracklen. The intrigues followed him here, to the already troubled Earth.

Chapter Six

Finally, after weeks of battling a demon and greeting an old enemy from Draxxt, as well as trying to keep up his salon business, Timothie felt a holiday was long overdue. He talked it over with Pauline and Skye, who agreed to keep the business open while he was gone. He pulled his phone from his pocket and googled vacation spots.

Although the exchange rate on the Canadian dollar was prohibitive, Timothie still had friends in the U.S.A. and places to visit on the dreams he yearned to fulfil. Las Vegas, "the entertainment capital of the world," was high on his list. Exodus Festival tickets were on sale, and he considered buying a Wolf Pack for men, but the price was high and Timothie ordinarily shunned crowds and loud groups of people. A vacation in Las Vegas gave him an idea, though, for the nearby state of Arizona.

"The Grand Canyon!" he announced, and Skye peeked in from the back salon to discover the source of this new excitement. Timothie's fingers flew over his Android phone as he found the information he sought. There was a bus from Las Vegas to the Grand Canyon, leaving from the Strip to Grand Canyon Village and a tour of the south rim, including the Hoover Dam Bypass. Lunch was included, plus free pick-up and drop-off at his hotel. The bus tour would cost less than eighty dollars American and took under two hours to get to the Grand Canyon.

That was it! His vacation goal! He could even fly to Palm Springs from Phoenix if he cared to, but he thought he didn't have time for a vacation that long. He'd be satisfied with a Las Vegas show, maybe a visit to a casino, and the Grand Canyon.

Quickly, Timothie scrolled through his appointments for the next week and called his first client to reschedule. "Do you mind, luv?" he asked Maude, the witch. "I so need a holiday."

"Of course, I don't mind, dear," the older woman said. "By the way, I love my purple spikes!"

"Knew you would." Timothie doodled on his phone as he spoke. "They're you."

"Enjoy your vacation," Maude said. "We can all wait until you get back."

Next, he called Mrs. Cardinal, who squealed with excitement when he told her where he was going. "That's so exciting, Timothie! Why, Gordon and I thought we'd take that tour as well, maybe soon. We've been there three times and seen something different on the rim every time. Arizona is wonderful!"

He agreed and, after a couple more calls, set down the phone. He closed the salon early that afternoon and went to his bank, where he withdrew a thousand dollars in American cash.

Paula was drinking coffee by the French press when he returned. "Is your passport up to date?" she asked. "Do you have a room booked?"

"Yes and yes, and I'm on standby with WestJet for Las Vegas tomorrow morning."

"You move fast, I must say."

Timothie grinned and pressed his right hand onto his stubbled cheek. "You have no idea!" he teased as his gym bag squirmed. His mobile phone played "Dixie."

"Timothie Hill," he answered.

"This is the MGM Grand confirming your room tomorrow night."

"Crazy Jack?"

The phone squeaked. "I don't like that name, old friend. How about you call me Dareboy?"

"How'd you find out my plans so soon? I just found out myself."

"ZAP! Gotcha, superhero."

Timothie closed down his mind, as he had learned to do with Mindbender. "I forgot you can read minds, Crazy Jack Dareboy."

Crazy Jack laughed, his voice high. "How'd you do that, Superman? Oh, yes. I know. Mind control, like on Minth – or Draxxt, as your plebeian friends would call our old planet. Do you ever miss home?"

"All the time." Timothie polished one brown military boot with a burgundy handkerchief. "How'd you get involved with the Fairy Queen, Dareboy? Only the fairies call our planet Minth."

"The fairies have been on that planet since time began. Not so with humans or their offspring, the Trolls and Picts. So Minth it was in the beginning and Minth it is now. I've lived with the Fairy Queen until the fairies threw me out. Learned their language, learned that the planet is really theirs. Not that I care."

Timothie considered. "Has anything changed there except the grab for power for the throne?"

"No. Just the usual cutthroat and wars."

"I thought Peace and Hope were the lay of the land since the old King died."

The phone squawked. "Not on your flying carpet. Humans won't change."

"Aren't you human, Dareboy?"

"Of course. That's why I am the way I am. I'm not essentially bad. It's in my DNA." Crazy Jack laughed. "My parents, of course, think differently. They exiled me to Fairyland. The dorks."

Timothie considered again. "Isn't that your grandfather's DNA? The old King Hakor was a violent man."

"Wait. You calling me violent?" Crazy Jack snorted. "Anyhow, toodle-oo, Mindbender the Second. I recognize that misfit's thumbprint on your brain. See you in Arizona."

"Wait–" The phone clicked and went dead.

Darn. He wouldn't be safe even thousands of miles from home. Timothie felt rather than heard the thrust of great wings against the windows of his salon. He glanced out and saw the Angel of the West, broad chest and billowing pinions pressed against the glass, a kind yet fierce gaze on Timothie's form in the silver chair. The Angel blew him a heavenly kiss, and Timothie relaxed.

Everything would be all right. Dareboy climbs buildings and leaps chasms. But Uriel and I can fly higher and faster. He counted the American bills. There was enough for a spot of gambling tomorrow night. Perhaps a diet Pepsi and Mexican food in the MGM lounge and an early night with room service the morning after he arrived, before the bus picked him up to take him to the Grand Canyon. Maybe even some wine. It was a special occasion.

He thought of the movie where Thelma and Louise drove over the south rim of the Grand Canyon. What a way to go! He knew the filming location was Dead Horse State Park and not the Grand Canyon, but still, the south rim was the destination of his coach tour in a couple of days, and unlike the film and many suicides since, he had no intention of driving over the edge. He would enjoy himself.

His phone trilled "Dixie" again. He glanced at the caller's number, seeing that it was blocked. He knew without answering that Dareboy was on the other end. He continued to close his mind, rose to his booted feet, tucked his purple shirt into his skinny Levi 510s, and strode out the door with his gym bag in his hand. Before locking up for the night, Timothie noticed that the wind had picked up and the sidewalk sign had blown over. He took the sign inside. Glancing at the dark skies, he felt a tug on his shoulder and grinned as he recognized the Angel of the West holding out her magnificent arms. Gratefully, Timothie donned his cloak and slipped into the warm embrace of his Angel.

Who needs WestJet? He thought as he catapulted to Ada Boulevard and his rooms on the upper front floors of the old Victorian mansion with the river view. Luckily, he had walked to work that morning, and his red 1967 Volvo 123 remained in the carport. He checked it over just in case some malcontent like Dareboy had trifled with one of his prized possessions. His sports car shone all chrome trim and metallic paint in the evening light. His car was safe, and so was Timothie in the arms of his Angel from heaven.

Chapter Seven

The WestJet flight to Las Vegas was like a dream trip; the only seat available resided in Plus Class. The complimentary food and bottles of water were more than sufficient for the three-hour flight. Timothie strode off the plane at McCarran Airport with his single carryon black and silver Gucci bag in his sinewy hand.

He'd had time to set up roaming on his phone before the trip. From the airport, he checked into the hotel with his mobile to avoid the check-in lines and called the concierge to book a spa for that night. The free shuttle brought him to the MGM Grand Hotel on the Strip within ten minutes. From his room, he made arrangements for the bus to the Grand Canyon to pick him up from his hotel on his third day. Later, wrapped in a thick white cotton robe, he watched all-night television movie channels, sipped on bottled water and ice from a small fridge in his room, and slept the sleep of the righteous in a luxurious pillow-top king bed in his west wing room.

He stayed in Las Vegas only two days but, during that time, had brunch and played blackjack at the Hard Rock Casino, laughed (because he'd seen it all before with Maude on Draxxt) at David Copperfield's magic tricks and fantastic show at the MGM Grand, and, best of all – enjoyed himself at the Flex Cocktail Lounge with drag shows, karaoke, and gaming. There he met up with a familiar face.

"Well, hello there, handsome." The lithe male figure in a khaki jumpsuit from Dickie's leaned on the bar quaffing a tequila spritzer with grapefruit juice. Condescending and young, his voice carried over the karaoke singers to the table where Timothie sat sipping on a diet Pepsi with a new Italian-American friend. He enjoyed the soda, knowing he wouldn't sleep well that night with caffeine floating in his system but, at that moment, not caring.

Timothie's voice rose above the gamers and karaoke in the room. "Crazy Jack," he said. "What the heck are you doing here, you little shit?"

His Italian-American companion excused himself from the table as Dareboy strolled over and plunked himself in the seat next to Timothie. "Miss me yet?" he asked and raised his tequila glass in a mock salute.

"No!" Timothie grimaced. "I don't want you here at all. Go crawl back under the maggoty rock you came from."

"Is that any way to treat an old flame? I thought we might hang out together before you leave on the tour coach tomorrow morning at ten. Funny, I've always wanted to see the Grand Canyon. Now's our chance, right, pal?" Dareboy smacked Timothie between the shoulder blades. The stylist's muscular body tensed.

"I'm leaving in the morning. Alone." He glanced around at the crowded room, but his new friend was nowhere. His hot, bloody heart beat as slowly as an athlete's beneath his muscular chest. On stage, a drag show started. The ladies were tall and tanned, festooned in feathers and tights – the band was loud, syncopated, and brilliant, the jokes corny but hilarious, Timothie thought as he sipped at his drink. Dareboy leaned closer, face next to the stylist's cheek.

"How do you like me so far?" he crooned. Timothie smacked down his glass and stood up.

"It's late," he said. "The tour bus picks me up at ten in the morning, outside the MGM Grand. Coming with me or not, Jack? I don't care, my dear."

The next morning, Timothie, in a white Fruit of the Loom tight tee-shirt and a pair of white Diesel low-rise jeans, wearing buckskin Blundstone boots, slouched on the luxury bus next to Crazy Jack Dareboy on their way to the Grand Canyon's south rim. He wasn't surprised when they stopped for lunch that Dareboy strolled away on the arm of a young caddy traveling with an older golfer. He wasn't surprised at his absence when they parked on the side of the south rim and gasped at the surreal drop of painted red, coral, and purple striped sandstone, shale, and limestone to the bottom. The Colorado River snaked like a silver ribbon past the indigenous village, the tiny horses and tourists, through the miles-long chasm cut through six million years of erosion.

Timothie rummaged in his bag for his Bushnell binoculars and peered at the bottom, over a mile below. The sun burned overhead and struck a rainbow of colors from the sedimentary rock that sloped in purple and red toward the base of the mighty cliffs. They stopped at several spots along the south rim and walked out onto the rocks which were protected by fences. Tourists stepped dangerously close to the sides.

"Stand down!" shouted the tour bus operator, but the young tourists paid no attention. Timothie snapped dozens of pictures with his phone camera. The tour operator snapped a photo of Timothie with the caddy and the older golfer. Dareboy seemed to have disappeared again.

"Jack!" The super stylist didn't really care if his old friend and nemesis was on the trip or not, as Crazy Boy had invited himself, but he still wouldn't want to see anything bad happen to the little jerk. They had a history together, after all, that stretched back to some alien planet lightyears away that swung around three suns and herded four moons, in a fantastical world of magic and danger. They shared a lot that no one on Earth ever knew or cared about. Timothie was lonely for his old friends. Dareboy was the closest he had come to a companion from Draxxt, and especially the country of Gracklen, since he landed near Vancouver ten years ago. The metal casing that carried him in fire and smoke from Mindbender's world was buried in a settlement of caves in the Coast Mountains, almost impossible to discover because of the magic and science used as camouflage.

So Timothie thought.

The tour bus stopped again and the guide distributed bottles of spring water to the group. Timothie explained Dareboy's absence as best he could, but he was beginning to worry.

"He's left the group. Went down in the valley by himself. He'll be all right. We're not coming back on the return trip, anyhow, as we plan to go to Phoenix this afternoon, and then head west to Palm Springs. Don't worry about him, sir."

However, the superhero was very worried. He spotted tiny figures a mile below, and one looked very familiar. The binoculars brought his form closer, a dark-skinned boy in a khaki jumpsuit and – what? – gun? – below on the bottom with the tiny horses and the tourists. Well out of the way of the indigenous village, he moved in a threatening fashion by the river which wound with serpentine languor between the mighty thighs of the cliff.

The human figures below were milling in an agitated fashion as though being herded by the boy with the – was it a gun? The noon sun blazed on a patch of snow. Timothie positioned his aviator sunglasses on his face. The river, Timothie knew, emptied into tributaries and estuaries beyond the canyon. It supplied fresh drinking water to many cities, including Phoenix and Los Angeles. He peered again through the binoculars, trying to focus more clearly, then threw the binoculars back in their case with a huff and burned the distance between with his radiographic eyes, not caring if anyone saw him. The figure below focused on the river, and Timothie could see the water boil and turn red.

He grabbed his bag from the bus and ripped it open. The Cloak of Power covered his back. It whipped in the desert wind, billowing around his head and shoulders. He wrapped himself in the black and silver stars of the fabric then launched himself off the side of the cliff before anyone could stop him, tight white tee-shirt and low-rise jeans a blur like snow descending.

"Stop that man!"

"Oh, no, Alfred, another suicide!"

"Oh, shit," cursed the coach operator who had brought them this far.

Down spiraled Timothie the superhero, cloak whipping in a fierce current of air as he dropped more than a mile to the bottom of the canyon, his feet closed together like an arrow or a spear. The forms of the tourists below grew larger; he could make out their features and hear the frightened screams. Dareboy held a long cattle prod in his hands which sparked with electricity. The Colorado River swirled and rose in great gulping torrents toward the southwest side of the canyon before flowing into Lake Mead and down to the Arizona-Nevada boundary. Why Dareboy wanted to divert the flow and poison the river was a matter of vicious DNA inherited, perhaps, in mindless violence from his grandfather the old King Hakor. There seemed no logical reason for his insane stirring of the river by the gargantuan electrical prod, the magic head of which spewed torrents of blood and mud into the stream.

"Maude, come here," Timothie called, spotting a familiar purple spiked head among the tourists in the bottom of the canyon. There were perhaps fifteen or twenty of them, milling about, screaming, as the river raged and turned blood red, erupting into torrents. A horrific waterspout formed to catapult its contents skyward. He noticed George and Clara Cardinal, clients from his spa, gaping at the sight. What were his clients doing here? The world was certainly turned upside down.

"He's poisoning the river," whispered Maude, gripping Timothie's elbow with a strong, gnarled hand. "He'll poison the drinking water of every city and town along its route, including Phoenix."

"That's the idea," yelled Crazy Jack Dareboy. His maniacal laughter strung out over the valley. His laughter and shouts echoed from the gorgeous sandstone cliffs all around. The river boiled. Mud and blood erupted. Timothie thought fast, as only he could do when wearing the magic Cloak of Power.

The superhero sprang onto a white horse nearby, dug his heels into the pony's sides, and careened bareback toward the crazy figure in the jumpsuit. Adjusting his sunglasses, he drew from his side a silver sword, suddenly at hand, and knew without a doubt that the Angel of the West galloped with him to the poisoned waters of the Colorado River. The river had etched its design for six million years into the cliffs around it, patiently carving the Grand Canyon. Now the river churned and boiled. The river was dying.

The white horse charged, foam flecking its nostrils, and Timothie rode it into the middle of the boiling waters. He plunged his sword into the heart of the river. A mighty vortex arose; a scream and hissing like lobsters boiling multiplied thousands of times over. The river erupted into hailstones, blood, and mud, then drained silently through a chasm in its bedrock, not there five minutes before. Timothie's sword slashed and tore at the fetid waters until they ran clear and crystal again. Any impurities drained into a gargantuan whirlpool that sucked through the bedrock and into the underworld. The river cleansed itself and flowed sedately once again, snaking along the bottom of the mighty canyon toward Lake Mead where it would water many towns and cities before flowing south to the international border into Matagorda Bay on the Gulf of Mexico.

The horse panted, slathered in sweat and foam dripping from its jaws around the bridle. Timothie threw the ends of the rope across its neck. He bounded to the earth, where Maude waited with the terrorized group of tourists.

"You had something to do with it," he said to Maude. "With the cleansing of the river, I mean. With the taming of the magic prod that my old friend wielded so viciously."

"The people of this Earth don't deserve that treatment," Maude replied. "Our planet is rife with magic and violence. We mustn't bring that to the children of this world."

"Yes, they are children," Timothie mused. He rubbed down the horse's sweaty sides with a corner of his cloak. He could see the small tribe of indigenous peoples watching them from below the cliffs. The tourists ran to their mules and horses and began to climb the long trail up the chasm. Clara Cardinal strode over to where Maude and Timothie stood.

"I saw it all," she said, her liquid brown eyes pooling with sympathy. "My people predicted this many moons ago. I think their spirituality and magic – yes, magic – helped you." Her husband, George, grasped her hand and pulled her to the bottom of the trail where their horses waited.

"The Great Spirit told us you needed us here," she continued. "You need all the good from every culture and nation on Earth to help you with this task, Timothie. We know about the mind controls you have yet to see, emanating from the evil that Reginald unleashed. We've seen their power, and in a dream, I have seen much of their evil."

She pressed Timothie's shoulder and moved away. "We'll be in touch back home. If you need my people, we will help. Many of our elders are old and wise. My George is one."

"The Great Spirit chose to make me ugly," George said. "Not stupid."

Timothie smiled his crooked grin. "Thank you, darlings. Now go on home. Quick. It's not safe here."

"Where is Crazy Jack?" Maude asked, taking the rope and leading the white horse back up the trail. "We took our eyes off him, and he's gone again."

"Yes." Timothie heard the rush of mighty wings. No one could see it except him, but sometimes someone would catch a glimpse and know the power that was there. Maude stared and stopped to listen. The Angel soared upward, not being needed anymore, and Timothie shoved his sword back in its scabbard. His white jeans were streaked with sweat and horsehair. He knew his bag was safe at the top where he had left it. He caught a glimpse of wings covering the south rim a mile above and leaped into the air, caught a gust of desert wind, and ascended swiftly to the top. No one noticed his rise to the rim above or saw him land there on his buckskin boots. So long as the great white pinions covered his tracks, he remained invisible and silent.

He shoved the Cloak of Power and the sword back into his bag. He was so angry with his vicious opponent who engaged in mindless violence against an innocent people that he didn't even check with the tour operator before launching himself at the Grand Canyon Village where he took a shuttle to the Grand Canyon Airport.

"A one-way ticket to the Phoenix Sky Harbor Airport," he ordered after arriving at the airport in Tusayan. "Please, dear, hurry."

He had decided on a whim to go to Palm Springs, so near and so appealing in its laid-back charm and enchanting history of the houses of Old Blue Eyes, Sammy Davis Jr, and others in the past. Its romantic history lent credence to its many museums, the bars and nightclubs, and the golfing and swimming. Timothie could enjoy a bit of each before heading home to Edmonton again. Now his vacation had turned sour and he didn't have the sense of peace or rest that he sought before leaving Edmonton.

He shoved the thought of Dareboy into a corner of his mind and focused on the Sky Harbor Airport coming up, his small plane circling, and his cloak stirred in his carryon Gucci bag. After a quick meal at the Barrio Café in Terminal 4, Timothie bought his ticket to Palm Springs. One hour and five minutes later he strode forth into the bustling regional airport. He rented a white Kia Rio compact car at Alamo Rent-a-Car and drove to the Hyatt Palm Springs hotel. He checked in and dined at Hoodoo's, then, exhausted, flung himself on his king bed in the chic room he'd rented and slept.

Much later that night, Timothie awoke refreshed and dialed room service. After the concierge delivered his taquitos and diet Pepsi, the superhero showered and shaved.

There were a lot of gay bars in downtown Palm Springs. Timothie dressed in a tight black tank and black Diesel low-rise jeans then strolled down E Tahquitz Canyon Way to Legends of Palm Springs. He checked his phone for the time. The blue backlight snapped on; the digital time read just past midnight. Legends was open till two that night. He had two hours to have a good time.

"Hello, handsome." Crazy Jack Dareboy met him at the door.

Chapter Eight

WestJet flew directly to Edmonton from Palm Springs. Timothie sighed and relaxed in the window seat in Economy Class. His long legs were cramped under the seat ahead. He startled as his phone played "Dixie."

"Timothie Hill."

"It's Reg, Timothie. I'm at work at TopStrategy Marketing. They've made me marketing director."

"You must be doing something right." Timothie made doodles on the face of his phone. The flight attendant clucked when she saw his Gucci bag stored improperly under the seat.

"Is your phone in airplane mode, sir?" the attendant asked. "We're going to leave the ground soon. About your bag…" She gestured, and he shoved it further under the seat with his foot.

"Soon," Timothie said. "Reg, I've got to go. My plane's about to take off."

"Where are you?"

"Leaving Palm Springs. I'm on my way home."

"What I mean to tell you about the good news, the promotion, Tim, is that things are going my way now. You know how you called me a loser? No more, pal. I found the answer. Let's meet for lunch when you get home. How long's your flight?"

The flight attendant hovered at the side of the row. Timothie nodded at her and prepared to shut his Android "Three hours. But I've really got to go now. How about next Tuesday for lunch?"

"On me, pal."

"Right. Thanks, the Italian Bakery is open again. It's not far from the salon. Give Paula a call and have her write it in for Tuesday at one."

"See you then." The phone went dead. "Keep your enemies close," his mentor on Draxxt had advised the young Timothie, "where you can keep an eye on them."

Timothie clicked *Airplane Mode* and began to watch a movie he'd downloaded. The flight attendant smiled and moved away. His movie flickered. There was interference, possibly from the cockpit, and possibly he shouldn't be watching a movie right now. Timothie frowned. He'd seen Avatar some zillion times already, anyhow.

Last night had gone well, his last night in Palm Springs after three days of adventure in gay bars, museums, and Mexican restaurants with the ever-present Crazy Jack Dareboy. Dareboy had proven invaluable because he could read minds. Crazy Jack, who drank Tequila and lime juice for the rest of the vacation. Timothie, drank the occasional glass of wine and diet Pepsi. He enjoyed a karaoke song and found that the hulking Italian-American, who had followed them to Palm Springs, had a pleasantly smooth baritone voice. Timothie didn't hook up with anyone else for the remainder of his vacation and allowed himself to be chased. The experience was rather satisfying.

On his last day there, "Big Chuck," Crazy Jack, and he took in a drag show at Toucans Tiki Lounge. "Big Chuck" got drunk, and they had a fight, and Crazy Jack announced to Timothie later, with a murmur into his tanned ear, that "Big Chuck" had a wife and child back in La Quinta near the Santa Rosa Mountains.

"Story of my life," Timothie sighed. "You can't trust gay men. They're all the same."

Crazy Jack laughed. "Another thing. That pretty boy bartender over there?"

"Yah?"

"He's got the hots for you."

Timothie smoothed his short-cropped salt and pepper hair with a tanned hand. “Not my type,” he said, paid for his Merlot, and left the bar.

Later, in the room he had booked for five days, he slouched in an armchair and clicked through the movies available on late night TV. Nothing interested him.

Thus, he sprawled in the window seat of his aircraft the next day, on his way to Edmonton. His Blundstone boots pressed against the black and silver bag jammed under the seat ahead. The earbuds he’d unfurled from his Android squawked a bit because the music was too loud. The attendant served him cold coffee. He had to pee. Nothing seemed right.

Then he thought of the salon waiting for him the next day and of his clients, including Maude with the purple spiked hair and Mrs. Cardinal and her bald husband, his shining pate useless to a hair stylist, he thought with a smile. Paula and Skye would have kept up his books and walk-in appointments. Uriel’s wings would be folded above the salon, keeping it a safe place for him in the midst of chaos surrounding him, Bael loose and Reginald moving up the corporate ladder with demonic assistance, no doubt.

Timothie sighed. His innate anxiety surfaced. The middle seat was empty, fortunately, for he had fallen asleep momentarily and his right hand drooped across the armrest next to him. The aisle seat was occupied by a middle-aged man with a laptop. Timothie glanced over at the glowing screen.

“I’m bored,” he said out loud. The man in the aisle seat grunted. “Excuse me,” Timothie continued, unhooking his seatbelt. The man grunted again and got into the aisle, allowing Timothie access to the bathroom in the back. As he stumbled past a view of the wings and the muted roar of the engines, Timothie pondered his fate. At thirty-five thousand feet in the air, the world below appeared magical through the clouds, shadows striking yellow fields of canola and shimmering lakes. Mountain peaks humped below in a panorama of brown, grey, and green patchwork, geology gone rampant, magic below and science above as the plane hummed homeward.

Magic and science would outwit Bael and his minion, Reginald. Magic and science would bring Timothie closer to the truth which he sought. Brushing past the man in the aisle, he settled into his seat and pinched his lower lip between his thumb and forefinger. The attendant collected the empty cups and wrappers. The seatbelt sign clicked on. He fastened his belt and thumbed the Android's movie channel. Idly, the tall green alien with the beautiful eyes swung on beautiful vines through beautiful jungles on the moon Pandora. *Great body*, Timothie thought, dreaming of science.

Science had brought him to Earth on the ancient refurbished rocket of his Draxxt-bound ancestors. Hidden in the Coast Mountains near Vancouver, the ancient metal "dragon" so revered by the Draxxians was covered with ash and cinder, unable to lift itself again to the heavens.

Timothie had narrowly avoided death on the descent to Earth. He would have to depend on magic to return to his country of Gracklen, but he may not ever go back. Earth was his home and his livelihood now. He had chosen with his mentor, the great Troll Mindbender, to return to the ancestral home of his people and help them overcome the doom foretold in the ancient books. The blessing he received in Gracklen before he left followed him to Earth, rendering him an unknown and unappreciated man but graced by God himself and the Angel He had sent to protect and nurture him.

Timothie was eager to return to his salon. Great things awaited him there, he was sure. Draxxt, which swung around the star Alpha Centauri B, was a distant memory of his childhood. Adrenaline poured into Timothie's muscular body. His barrel chest heaved. He glanced at his Android, where the Na'vi swung through trees and jungles on the exoplanetary moon Pandora, mined by ruthless humans, so like reality. He determined to change that reality for humanity. Slowly, the reason for Uriel's interest in him gathered courage and depth, and he understood, or almost, his destiny, tied to Reginald and the demon, tied to Maude and Mindbender, the Fairy Queen, and Dareboy.

Timothie was special. He could no longer deny the reality. His search for truth had led him here. Reginald's rise in the corporate world of marketing mirrored Timothie's understanding and mystical entwinement with the destiny of the world – Asia, Africa, Europe, the Americas, and Oceania came to mind as continents threatened by hunger, poverty, crime, natural disasters, climate change, wars, and ultimately, total annihilation.

Sunlight spilled through the small round window of the Boeing 767-300. He pulled down the blind. He settled his aviator sunglasses on his face and perused the face of the Android. The protagonist, Jake Sully, lay prone on the rock, awaiting his resurrection at the end of the movie *Avatar*. Timothie loved this part. He never tired of miracles, nor of good overcoming evil. It was why he had been born, he was sure, why his parents had to die so young in a senseless war on a faraway planet, leaving the small boy to be raised by a king and queen, and why even now the Angel's wings hovered with great white pinions of faith over the safe portal of Timothie Hill's Salon & Spa.

* * *

Reginald signed and chanted in secret. The pentagram swirled, and he focused once more on the black, white, and red form of the mighty demon from Hell who planned to enslave as many souls as possible and claim the throne of God. Reginald would help, his soul already enslaved and eager to skyrocket to the top of his corporate career with the newest trend in subliminal advertising. Reginald possessed a plan which was not only complicated (the Devil is in the details!) but diabolical in nature. The scheme would enslave the greatest number of souls possible in a way no one suspected, that would ensure the subjugation of all nations under a worldwide tyranny of pure evil.

* * *

His short flight from Palm Springs completed and home at last, Timothie gazed at the splendid view of the river valley from his rooms at the top of the Victorian style mansion on Ada Boulevard. Bands of peach and pink swelled across the southwestern skyline. Purple wings of cloud chased the setting sun into oblivion, casting long shadows, and finally darkness spread itself across the verdant valley. Lights like crystal stars burned in the towers on the hill opposite the river valley. Watching the breathtaking scenery, Timothie wondered offhand if he should sell his car. It seemed redundant now that he could fly.

An ad for a book on neuromarketing popped up on his Android. He flicked a switch on an Ikea floor lamp by his Cherrywood credenza and peered at the description of the book. An interesting and rather sinister concept, he thought. He wondered if Reginald had seen it.

Of course, he had.

Chapter Nine

Dressed in skinny, stretchy khaki jeans and a *Jaws* movie poster tee-shirt with a splash of red across the front, Timothie sat on the edge of his bed and pulled on his white Converse high tops. He yawned hugely, meandered into the kitchen, and plugged in the electric kettle. Next, he sipped on a cup of black coffee and checked on the cell his appointments for the day. Paula had reminded him of the lunch date with Reginald at one – as though he could forget. His first appointment was with Starr from Sapphire Designs down on Alberta Avenue, the woman with the rainbow extensions. He wondered if she wanted them removed and how her conference had gone with designers from across the continent. Paula had made her appointment, too. Then nothing until eleven o'clock, a simple haircut for Mrs. Cardinal with her black hair down to her hips. Reginald was booked for an hour from one to two in the afternoon. Maude would come in at 2:30 for a color and cut. So it went.

Timothie opened a box of oatmeal raisin cookies and chewed on two or three as he took the stairs down to the carport. He threw his bag into the back of his red Volvo and slid into the driver's seat. He buckled up and adjusted the rear-view mirror, and the sporty vehicle purred into the street with the superhero at the wheel. Ada Boulevard was quiet as usual, but when he reached the intersection of 112 Avenue and 50 Street past Highlands, he punched his right foot on the gas pedal, and the car sprouted silver wings. It soared into the air and glided to a stop behind his salon. He'd been gone for thirty seconds. Luckily, the cloak of invisibility nestled in his bag rendered the Volvo invisible as well.

Timothie grinned his crooked smile, rubbed the bristles on his handsome face, and strode into the back of Timothie Hill's Salon & Spa. Neither Paula nor Skye were there yet so he used his key. He poured boiling water into the French press by Skye's waiting room and drank a second cup of coffee while opening the blinds in the main area. Starr was early and waiting for him at the front door. He could see right away that she was like a rainbow dancing across the hardwood floors.

"Morning, beautiful," he greeted and beckoned her to the chair. "How do you like the hair extensions, dearie?"

Starr beamed. "They're fabulous, Tim. But…"

"What would you like me to do for you this morning?" He ran his fingers through the colored tresses. "Is it too much?"

"A little," she admitted. He removed about half of them, smoothed her shiny chestnut hair, and wove the remaining lime green, yellow, hot pink, and purple extensions into psychedelic locks around her face.

"How do you like your new digs?" she asked. "It's near Highlands, isn't it?"

"Yes. It overlooks Floden Park with a view of the 50th Street footbridge. Nice quiet old Victorian mansion right above the North Saskatchewan River. I've always loved that view. The lights on the other side of the river valley are wonderful at night, darling, and especially in the early morning hours in December and January. Love it."

"Did you buy it?"

"Yes, they've turned it into condos. I have the front rooms at the top. Cozy and convenient to the salon."

"I'm so glad you've moved away from that dreadful Reginald's place. He has money but no class. I couldn't ever see you with him."

"That reminds me," he said. "I'm seeing him at one. Chop-chop, dear. My next appointment's at eleven and I hear Skye in the back room. Sugaring today?"

"No, thanks. Just a hug. No music today?"

He strode across the room and lifted the top of the antique stereo. "But of course. Do you like Jann Arden?"

"You know I do."

"Another heartbreak song," Timothie said and lifted the arm of the turntable. "Insensitive." "Reminds me of my ex. The jerk."

"Reginald?"

"Who else?"

Starr swung her legs to the floor. The mirror swayed from the silver chain. "Get over it, Tim."

"Oh, how do you think I can do that? You know what they say, keep your enemies close where you can keep an eye on them. My old mentor used to tell me that. A wise man."

She paid him with a credit card. "So, now Reginald is your enemy?"

"He wasn't always."

"Lovers change," she said and hugged him again. "See you in six weeks."

Timothie gazed at his Android. "He's never been into the salon in this location. Doesn't know how it's fixed up, how I work, if I'm okay, nothing. Paula and Skye have never met him. He's changed a lot. For the worse."

"I know." She winked. *What does she know*? He heard the door close, and a gust of wind whooped down 118 Avenue. His next appointment was almost due. He sighed and poured himself another cup of coffee from the vintage Bodum. Paula and Skye peeked in from the back spa rooms and greeted him.

"We missed you," Paula said. "So did your friends."

"What friends?" he looked up from his mobile phone, which glowed blue and colored his world happy.

Skye leaned on the side of the stereo. "Insensitive"… "Someone came to see you when you were gone."

"Who?"

"Why, the guy that cracks his knuckles. Had a crazy look in his eye. Didn't like him at all. He asked about you then, when I turned around, he was gone."

Timothie shuddered. "I'm meeting him for lunch," was all he said. *Bael.*

Chapter Ten

Timothie flexed the wiry muscles in his forearms and settled the Cloak of Power around his neck. Time enough to check on Reginald with his radiographic vision before the lunch, to see what his former friend was up to before the actual appointment. After the last client of the morning was sent on her happy way, Timothie bounded through the suddenly soluble windows and roared skyward, searching the city for signs of Bael.

Far below, wisps of cloud and sunshine crawled over Edmonton's landmarks as Timothie scanned them for signs of Reginald or his demonic allies. Reginald had inherited his fortune from a distant uncle with no heirs, had paid a million dollars easy for the penthouse suite in the Oyster, but toiled in an ad agency by day for recognition from his peers. He had left them behind in spending but was intellectually still their equal. They called him Bootjack Smith at work, a parody of a television sitcom.

Reginald could have been a superhero, too, thought Timothie, twirling in midair on one perfectly fitted navy and white Converse shoe. His skinny low-rise navy-blue jeans and navy polka dot tee-shirt were almost hidden beneath the billows of the star-spangled cloak. Magic winds whistled past his ears and there – he saw it – a tower of fire in the penthouse in Oliver!

Reginald was hunched over the wheel of a yellow Lamborghini exiting the underground parking at the Oyster. Forty stories above his churning tires, he had left the demon chewing great chunks of lava from Hell below and bellowing for the souls of a billion humans to complete its deadly mission. Timothie saw the luxury car twinkle in an instant and reappear at the gates of the Olde Towne of Beverley, just two blocks from his salon.

He inhaled and flashed toward their designated meeting place at the Italian Bakery. His Angel met him with folded wings and took the cloak from his shoulders, stuffing it into the bag that nestled on the counter in front of the salon's wide windows.

Lightly Timothie tapped onto the pavement by the sign outside his building. He scanned the area with his radiographic vision. The Lamborghini sat parked two blocks away. A siren ululated along 118 Avenue. *Ask not for whom the bell tolls*, he thought. *It tolls for me.* He smiled his wry and crooked smile and almost danced down the street toward the Italian Bakery.

When the superhero arrived, he found Reginald seated at a small table. "Hola," Timothie said and pulled out a chair. He ordered a latte and a Cobb salad, and Reginald opened a slim briefcase.

"You probably wonder why I called," Reginald began. He rubbed the side of his face with a pale hand. He bit into his sandwich.

Timothie's stomach lurched. "No, I think I know. You've unleashed a power you can't control. You want me to help."

Still chewing, Reginald set down his sandwich. "That's not it, exactly. You know and I know there are powers that are beyond us mortals. I want to tap into that power. Ever since that little weasel, Crazy Jack Dareboy, moved in on us from the new planet you both left, I've been thinking about Bael's proposition."

"Which is?" Timothie munched on his salad. It was excellent; the egg was boiled just right, the way he liked it. He covered his mouth with his hand and swallowed. The latte also was the best he'd ever tasted.

Reginald burped. "He wants human souls. No damn problem. What's it to me what happens in the Heavens after we're all gone? The Earth is headed for a major meltdown anyhow, either nuclear or environmental.

We all know that. Our leaders are either helpless or helping the destruction along its way. I think Bael has more friggin' souls than he knows what to do with, confidentially, but he needs an army. I don't give a fig about that, Tim. It's nothing to me what this demon wants in the afterlife. Hell, I didn't even believe in the afterlife until I met Bael. Crazy Jack gave me this book, see, and while we were, er…cohabiting, Jack and me, well, I sort of borrowed the kind of vocabulary needed, and the tools, to create this monster from the pentagram in my floor tiles. Which in itself is a pretty odd story. The pentagram, that is." He paused to take another bite of the European ham and cheese sandwich. "Mmmm," he continued. "Delicious."

"So?" Timothie leaned forward, his salad forgotten. He toyed with the latte, drawing circles on the wet tablecloth with his forefinger.

"So, it just appeared one day on the blue tiles, near the drain that also appeared."

"Was that before or after you and Dareboy got fooling around with the spells?"

Reginald guffawed and leaned back in his chair, splitting his briefcase open on the table in front of him. His laptop glowed blue even in the bright lights of the little coffee shop.

"You're smart, my friend. It was about that time, I remember the day, about two weeks before Dareboy went back to his rooms at the Abbotts Manor downtown. About two weeks before he left, that is, and it's my fault, I suppose. I drove him out same as it was my fault you left, Tim."

"Never would have thought you'd admit it," Timothie drawled. He picked up his fork again.

"I got something here, though," Reginald said. "It's in this life, not in that friggin' afterlife the demon keeps on about. I told you I got a promotion? I'm director of the R&D department now. And I got an idea. More than one idea, actually, which is why they like me so much."

"So?"

"So, you read about this neuromarketing? I sent you a link last week."

"Yeah, I read about it. Thought it was pretty sinister; thought it was something you'd be interested in. More than subliminal advertising, using the brain to get at the clients' buying habits and, more than that, control, my old budderoo. Control. That would be you. Yes, I read it."

Reginald leaned forward. "It's more than that. It's control, yeah. You're right. Control of the whole damn world, bud! I got something here; working on a patent. My company's really hush-hush about it, but it works in with Bael's plans just hunky dory."

"So why are you telling me about it?" Timothie finished his latte and looked around. He checked his watch. It was almost time for his next appointment, and Reginald seemed intent on telling him this latest hare-brained scheme of his. Timothie sighed. He'd heard them all. But neuromarketing – now that seemed something right up Reginald's toilet, if anything ever was. Maybe he was interested.

"Because I want you in on it, pal." Reginald dropped his voice. "You've got Dareboy on your side. I'm afraid I alienated that little son of a two-barrelled shotgun a long time ago. He won't work for me. But he'd be on our payroll if you said the word. I want you. I want your creativity, I want your clients, I want to pick your brain. Most of all, I want your superpowers. I want that friggin' Angel I saw. I want the magic that comes from that planet you come from. You can help, and I'm not sure I can do it without you."

"I'm not interested," Timothie said. He scratched his ribs. His feet pointed toward the door.

"I know, I haven't told you what's in it for you. Yet."

"So, what's in it for me?"

"Power, Tim. Riches beyond your imagination. Together, we can control the world. This neuromarketing, it will just scratch the surface. We need to sell this thing."

Timothie sighed. "I don't care about power or riches. I want what's right."

"Don't get on your high pockets with me. Everybody wants to be rich. Everybody wants power."

"Not me."

Reginald leaned closer, his breath stinking in Timothie's face. "You want a new salon and spa in Riverdale? Done. You want your girls taken care of for life? Done. You want your mother and father back from the dead? Done, done, and done. Bael can do anything. You can't imagine. All you have to do in return is work with me on this soul thing."

"Soul thing?" Timothie asked. Prepared to get up, he leaned forward in his chair and planted his navy and white runners on the rungs.

"Yeah. We deliver all the souls on Earth to Bael, so he can recruit an army strong enough to be God Almighty – what's it to us? – and we have immortality, unlimited wealth, unlimited power. You think my penthouse is astonishing? Wait 'til you see what's in it for you. Anything your heart desires, my friend, will be yours. You want that pretty boy or that pretty girl down the street, you want designer clothes, you want gold bullion sitting in a bank vault for your old age, you want old age, do you? Anything you want, all you gotta do is plant these things on unsuspecting humans, and they'll do our will."

"The demon's will." Timothie's voice was flat. "Evil can be changed to good. I believe in the basic goodness of mankind. You lost me a long time ago, Reg."

"No, you don't understand. It's a new software, a game that'll go viral; everybody will be playing it. Dareboy knows it's magic, but he backed off when he saw the potential. It takes special 3D glasses, you see, and they're wired directly to the brain. This neuromarketing is brilliant, I tell you. They'll sell their souls for a chance to keep playing this game. It's going viral this very moment, Tim. You just haven't heard about it yet. It started out with the kids; now the Millennials are picking it up. You're the last generation to know about it."

Timothie grimaced. "I'm disgusted. Why are you telling me this now?"

"Why now? Because it's not working out the way we thought. We need your magic, Tim. We need Dareboy's daring. The kids are great, yeah, it's going viral, but for the wrong reasons. They're using it to help their studies, they're using it to get girlfriends and boyfriends, they're using it to connect. We don't want them to connect. We want them to fly away like Peter Pan into never-never land. It's not another Pokemon. We want them to lose their souls."

"Somebody mentioned it a couple of weeks ago. It might be going viral if Clara and George Cardinal know about it already. The mind controls. I'm not having any part of it," Timothie declared. "And I don't see how it can be done with a game."

"Oh, we have the software," Reginald responded. "Last time Bael took over my body, we went to the V.P. of my company and pitched it. The company's working on it, and the prototype is out. Like I said, it's going viral with the kids. They're sharing it like they should. Internet cafés are springing up, dedicated to this new game."

"What do you call it?"

"Don't have a name for it, yet. That's another thing. It needs a name that sounds like it's something for the good of mankind, you know, like Millennial Goggles or something. Right now, it's called Prototype B."

Timothie stretched, and his shirt with the sleeves cut off popped a seam. "Sounds catchy."

"Don't be sarcastic," Reginald said. "We need to control this. Otherwise, it will be just another craze. Of course, my V.P.s and marketing people don't know about the end result, and of course, they wouldn't believe there was a Bael even if they saw him. But you and I know better."

"I think you don't have this under control," Timothie objected. "I think you need help, Reginald, and it's not for what you think. This game sounds like it's in another universe. It's something that's bigger than you and bigger than me, and Bael has a lot to do with it, I expect. This neuromarketing is trending now, and it just coincides with what you want to do with your new software. It's fiendish. My Angel is from God Himself, and we're on different teams you and I, that's for sure. Now take your viral game and make a lot of money with it, but don't try to buy souls. It won't work. Not in this life. Not as long as I'm here, or Crazy Jack, even. Though I don't know what he had to do with the start of it, I believe you, it would be just crazy enough for him. I know it's too much for him now, though, and he won't have anything to do with your fiendish scheme any more than I will. So, go to Hell." He stood up.

Reginald tapped a few keys on his laptop. "Here," he said. "I'll show you what I'm talking about."

"Yeah, you're talking about the whole world going to Hell in a handbasket," Timothie said. He put both hands on the sides of his face and frowned, his stubble prickly against the tender skin of his palms.

"No, this is it," Reginald objected. He passed the laptop over to his former friend and current superhero, who was now standing by his shoulder. Other lunch patrons had left. The big digital clock on the opposite wall flashed two p.m.

"I have to get back. I'm expecting a client at two," Timothie said. He glanced at the laptop screen, which flashed an intricate series of schematics for a hypothetical game that apparently would change the brains of its participants to willing slaves.

"I see what it's supposed to do, but I don't believe it in this life. Reg, what happened to you? What happened to us? Are power and fame really all that matters to you? And money? Don't you have enough?"

"There's never enough," Reginald objected. He slammed the laptop shut. "There, you've seen our projection of what this game can do. Of course, its ultimate goal is universal slavery, but my company simply thinks it's the next thing to go viral and will make us billions."

Timothie started to move away. "Which it might," he said. "Be satisfied with that. They'll make you President of TopStrategy Marketing, or Chairman of the Board. Be content. Accept, Reg. You can't win over billions of souls in the world for a demon that will destroy your soul. Ultimately. You can't do this. It won't be allowed. The universe won't allow it. Hell isn't that strong. Good always wins over evil."

"Oh, you're so naïve, Tim." Reginald sat with his face in his hands. "We'll figure this out. I know we will. There's more at stake here than you know." He looked up, and his eyes flashed, his mouth twisted, his breath came in stinking waves, and Timothie stepped back as his former friend cracked his knuckles and cackled. Fire began in the corners of the coffee shop, fire that spread rapidly, and Reginald fled with his laptop cradled in his arms. Outside, the Lamborghini farted and spurted beneath the town sign, then was gone.

Timothie spread his arms, and a puff of wind extinguished the blaze. No one noticed. Perhaps it was invisible to all but those from the magical realms of imagination and creativity, like a super hairstylist, an Angel of the West, or a demon from Hell.

Chapter Eleven

"Puh-leeze, Timothie, no more purple spikes," begged his client, Maude, as she sat in the silver chair two weeks later. Her reflection showed a tall older woman with tortoise shell eyeglass frames, a pink tee-shirt, and white capris. A complementary white denim jacket with brass buttons hung on the lobby hook. She wiggled her feet in the hot pink Under Armor runners. Maude was prone to fidget, and today was no exception. The mirror in front of her swayed with the tap of her foot. Her black and white Québec bag nestled at the foot of the chair, which Timothie had cranked to its lowest setting.

"Whatever you say, darling," he said, smoothing her tresses with a round brush. "Let's not do spikes anymore. I agree. What about this?" He flipped to a magazine page that showed a couple of older models, one with ash blonde hair cut in a pixie.

"Yes, I like that," she gushed. "It'll make me look my age. My hair just gets darker with every year that goes by. I'm like my mother, whose hair was still dark at ninety-one when she died. My lucky daughter has the same thing; she's a natural blonde, and no grey at all."

Timothie spread a cape around his client's wrinkled neck. "It's in the genes."

"I remember back on Draxxt..." Maude began, then stopped when Paula peeked around the corner of the salon. "Oh, hi. I didn't see you standing there, Paula. Are you still sugaring back there in the spa?"

"Oh, yes. I'm booked up for today, but would you like to make an appointment? I just came in to turn the music up. Ponchielli is my favorite."

"This is called the 'Hours Dance,' " Timothie whisked Maude to the sink in the back of the room and began to lather her hair. "My favorite, too." He began to hum. "Why don't we ever dance anymore, Paula?"

"Because you're always busy in the mornings," she said. "The old days were so much fun. So dreamy, dancing with you, Timothie. I miss that. What's happened? You're always so busy lately, and when you're here, you're preoccupied. Skye was wondering the same."

Timothie paused while shampooing Maude's hair. "Nothing personal. I know I've been absent quite a lot. A day in the life of an entrepreneur." He began to rinse his client's hair. "I can answer your question, darling. Yes, Paula does still sugar, and she has a new mirror and a quilt for her table, a crafty windchime and mobile, pretty soft lights, and pictures on the wall. The floors shine, and the walls are freshly painted. You'll love it."

"Sounds great," Maude said. She smiled at Paula. "Yes, make me an appointment, please, for next week sometime, around one."

Paula disappeared into the back, then returned momentarily with a book in her hands. "Tuesday all right for you, Maude?"

"Perfect." Maude cracked her knuckles.

Timothie dried Maude's hair with a spongy white towel and guided her back to the silver chair. Paula brushed past the coffee press and the white cups on her way to the back of the spa. The horse chestnut vines cascaded up the ladder that leaned against the east wall. Something moaned in the corner. As though caught in a brisk wind, the plants along that section of the room stirred and twisted in their pots. Timothie bipped and bopped to the "Hours Dance." Maude cracked her knuckles again.

"Odd," Timothie said. He began to run a plastic comb through Maude's hair.

"What, dear?"

"I have another friend who does that. A lot. And only when he's upset."

"Oh? What's that, dear?"

"He cracks his knuckles when he's possessed," Timothie observed. He turned his back and began to mix a bleach and color concoction. "How's this? It will be ash."

"Not blonde?"

"I don't like any yellow in my ladies' hair."

"That's perfect. It's just what I wanted. You're so smart, Timothie." Her breath washed over him like the fragrance of an ocean. "I was saying. When I knew you on Draxxt…"

He stirred the concoction and began to apply it to her hair. "We won't talk about that."

"No, I want to, Timothie. When I was on Draxxt, you know I sold charms and other magic stuff to the citizens of Gracklen and beyond? Even the fairies and Trolls were my clients. Indeed, the good Fairy Queen was a customer."

"I remember. But I was young then. I remember a fertility bracelet for our Queen and a black jade pendant for the King, her consort. She believed in them. That's all it took. Her fecundity is legendary now."

"Sometimes belief is all you need," agreed Maude. She studied her reflection in the hanging mirror. Timothie tied a plastic hood around her chin, and she choked. "That's a bit tight," she said.

"Sorry, luv." He adjusted it. "Yes, I know you were a healer on Draxxt."

"They called me a witch, actually," she corrected. She pulled her left earlobe and wrinkled her nose.

"Well, yes, but I wouldn't go that far."

"They did. I cursed them to Hell for it, too. I curse them now." Her voice rose.

Alarmed, the hair stylist set his timer and offered the first thing he could think of to calm someone, and that wasn't calm but loaded with caffeine.

"Would you like a cup of coffee or tea?" he asked. "I can make either one."

"That would be nice." Maude settled down and picked up her glasses. "I can't see without my glasses," she complained. "Maybe I could have something to read, if you don't mind? Something with pictures of hair, maybe, so I can get some ideas."

"Here you are." Timothie came back with a cup of black coffee and a magazine. "You'll like this. I thought I'd cut it shorter, in a pixie, and don't you dare spike it!"

"It's short enough now, but it has been growing out," she acknowledged. "That looks cute. Okay."

"I never asked you why you came back to Earth. I can imagine you weren't happy on Draxxt, though. You were relegated to a minor role, sitting in the market, selling gems and charms, and not respected by the customers who made good use of your knowledge and wisdom."

Maude flipped through the pages. "They called me a witch. I was, too, but an old woman mainly, who sat on the sidelines and wasn't respected. Here on old Earth, I have a job, a cool vintage car that still runs and isn't full of rust, thanks to its Western heritage where we don't salt the roads like they do in the East. I have friends. Nobody knows my history or cares. That's what's so cool about cities. You're anonymous." She smiled and pulled at her left ear. She winked and wriggled her nose.

"Yes, I like that, too," Timothie said. He wore a white dress shirt with the sleeves cut off to accommodate his bulging biceps. On his lower body were skinny Levi 510 jeans and black and white Converse runners. Outside, a young couple glanced in the window and stopped to read the sign. A few cars roared by. "I'm thinking of another holiday next long weekend in March," he continued. "Get away for awhile."

"That would be good for you," Maude agreed. She pointed to a picture in the magazine. "I like that one."

"That's exactly what I have in mind." He tested her hair for doneness, then motioned her to the sink again where he washed and rinsed the new color. "Don't look," he said.

After his customer settled under the dryer, Timothie took the coffee cups to the back room to clean them and returned them next to the stainless-steel vintage Bodum. It didn't make coffee hot enough, but it was acceptable. He hummed as CKUA began to experiment with alternative music and his favorite alternative band, Red Hot Chili Peppers, belted out "Californication" and "Otherside." He noticed that Maude tapped her foot to the beat. How could she hear the songs from under the whir of the dryer? Then he noticed the witch levitating two inches from the seat.

This isn't Maude, he thought and began to sweat. "Finished, dearie?" he asked out loud, testing her very short pixie cut and the ash color was fantastic and Maude's eyes were glowing, her skin turned greenish, her breath was like a red-hot furnace, and Timothie threw open his gym bag and called for the Cloak of Power.

He glanced out the window. A yellow Lamborghini was parked illegally just behind the blue 1979 Mercedes-Benz. Maude pressed cash into his palm. She threw off the salon's cape from around her wattled neck.

"Fantastic. Just what I wanted," she cackled. "Are you all right, Timothie? You look a little pale. And hey, I love that cape."

"It's a cloak," he protested, levitating six inches from the floor. Luckily, the girls in the back room were preoccupied with their customers and wouldn't notice his stunt. His cloak whipped with a sudden drop of air pressure in the room, which created a violent windstorm right in the salon. The gale stopped at the entrance to the back rooms, where the girls were presumably unaware of the drama playing out in the main salon.

Maude cracked her knuckles. She wrinkled her nose and pulled at her left earlobe. "Are those wings I see outside? I feel faint. I must get some air."

Timothie again glanced out the windows and saw the huge soft pinions of Uriel outlined against the backdrop of the traffic on the streets. In the salon, as well, feathers drooped in a protective hover over the room. "Thank the Lord," he whispered. "It's going to turn out good. Good always triumphs over evil."

"That's right," Maude said as she strode through the lobby and snatched her jacket from the hook. "You're not weak, Timothie. We misjudged you."

"We?" he asked. The outside door flew open and banged shut as if in one motion. The air pressure in the room rose again, and the windstorm was still, leaving only a dusting of gold and silver on the tools of his trade: the mirror, the silver chair, the combs and the colors. When he looked out again, the Lamborghini was gone. Appearing vulnerable and old, Maude leaned against the driver's side of the Mercedes. She vomited into the street.

Timothie swirled his black and silver-spangled cloak about the room, celebrating with the Angel of the West, celebrating with the Red Hot Chili Peppers as they sang their final song of the afternoon, "Jungle Man." He drove home in his cherry red Volvo 123 which sprouted silver wings to the mansion on Ada Boulevard where solitude awaited him.

Nowhere on the five-second trip home did he see the yellow Lamborghini or the baby blue Mercedes with the farting exhaust. He thought perhaps he'd won the day. "I'm gonna get me some bush," he sang and smiled his crooked smile. Bael had lost.

Not a bad day for a superhero.

Chapter Twelve

"Why are you wearing those goggles?" Timothie asked Skye two weeks later. In the back of the salon, she peered at her laptop.

"They're the latest craze." She smiled. "Everybody's wearing them."

"I'm not."

"They're sold exclusively through TopStrategy Marketing. A local company that's gone viral."

Timothie's stomach lurched. "How do they work?"

"It's a cool new game. Here, try them."

He grasped the yellow arms and noted the electrodes embedded in the frame. When he placed the goggles on his face, his brain exploded into millions of psychedelic pieces and fireworks. Then a pyramid appeared in three dimensions, maybe four, he thought, turning and whirling, and he asked, "What am I supposed to do with it?"

"All you have to do is use your mind," Skye said. "It's super cool. Put the pyramid into place in that background, where the whirlybirds are, and match the colors. That's all. It isn't easy, though."

"No, it isn't," Timothie agreed, removing the glasses. His mind whirled, and he saw after-images of the twirling pyramids and the colors. His hands itched to put the glasses on again. "It was only for a few seconds," he mumbled.

"What?" asked Skye, smiling and putting goggles on her face again.

"I wore them only for a few seconds, and I'm almost addicted," he explained.

"Oh, don't be silly. It's just a fun game. Everybody's playing it."

Timothie considered. "Does anyone ever win?"

"Oh, I think so. I don't know. That's not the point. The point is to have fun, to engage yourself in the psychedelic colors. It's almost as good as mushrooms."

"Better, I'd say," interrupted Paula, entering the room with her own pair of yellow goggles. The lenses were dark red and flashed into Timothie's eyes in an annoying fashion.

"Put those down," he ordered. "It's time to get to work."

"Don't tell us what to do," Paula said, giggling. She adjusted the glasses, and her mouth made an "O." "This is better than a party."

Timothie held out his arms. "Give those to me."

"No, what do you think you're doing? Who do you think you are? These are our personal items, and it's a game we paid for. It was cheap, too. Too cheap, if you ask me, for a game that's gone viral. I love it." Paula twirled as though she were at a ballet barre class.

"We can't stop thinking about it," agreed Skye. "Don't take away our new toys, Timothie, you spoilsport!"

"I'm thinking of you girls," he said. His brain whirled, retaining after-images. "I might know more about this new 'toy' than you do."

"Oh, it's just a game. A harmless game that's sweeping the country. Let us keep them."

Timothie's phone played "Dixie." He glanced at it and moved away. It was a London, U.K. call and could be only one fellow, Gianni Simoni, whom he'd known since he was sixteen. "Timothie here," he said and chuckled deep in his throat.

"Timothie!"

The assistants giggled and went back to their spas. Timothie meandered back to the salon and draped himself over the armchair in the corner. He spoke in excited tones to his old friend.

"It's so good to hear from you, Gianni! How have you been? How's London? Are you coming back anytime soon?"

"I was going to ask you that," replied Gianni. "How about visiting me here in my digs in London sometime soon? There's an Elton John concert and a big party afterward – you'd love it here, Timothie. Seen the Eye yet? A spectacular view of the city."

"I haven't been to England since you moved there a decade ago. I'd love to come visit. I've just been away. Give me two or three weeks, old buddy, and I'll join you." Timothie's mind raced. He wouldn't have to book a flight. He could fly! "I've got so much to tell you."

"Have you heard the latest craze? It's a new game. Just got here from the States, but I think the company is Canadian, if I'm not mistaken, old chap. Some place called TopStrategy Marketing."

"I heard about it." Timothie pulled on his lower lip. He frowned.

"Didn't our old friend Reginald Smith used to work for that company? Not that he needs to work, laugh out loud."

Timothie considered how much he should tell Gianni. "He still does. He had a lot to do with that new game of theirs that everyone seems to be talking about. Even you."

"You sound like you don't approve. It's quite addictive, I assure you."

"I know that."

"Have you seen the news?" Oh-oh.

"What? I don't watch a lot of television, you know that, and my online news is spotty lately. Too busy here making my own news, Gianni."

"I bet you are. I've known you since you first arrived, oh so mysteriously, in Vancouver at the age of sixteen. You were wet behind the ears, but didn't we have fun?"

"Fresh off another planet."

"Yes, hah, well, you sure seemed like it at the time. A naïve little gay boy, and in many ways, you still are, my friend. But in a delightful way."

"What are you doing with yourself now, dear?"

"Oh, I'm having fun as usual in jolly old England, working for the Establishment. A posh hotel group where I'm general manager. We have tons of fun. You ought to come see me, say, in February or March? Get you to God's country in the middle of friggin' winter."

"That sounds good. Gives me enough time to take care of business here. And Gianni?"

"Yes?"

"Be careful with those yellow glasses."

"How do you know what color they are?"

"We have them here," Timothie sighed. "My assistants in the spa in back are crazy about the new game, and they insisted I try it."

"Addictive, isn't it?"

"Yes. Addictive. I think they want to call it the Millennial Goggles, according to Reginald. And why do you want me to watch the news?"

"Very interesting. Nothing to do with anything personal, of course, but the leaders of all nations seem to have lost their minds."

"What's new?"

"No, I mean, really. It's scary. They're all talking peace."

"That's scary?" Timothie asked. He scratched his stubbly jawline.

"You should see it. Yes. They're all lining up under the United States government, which is threatening nuclear war if they don't come alongside. It looks like a universal government, under one tyrant. Ducksworth has done it this time, and his people, all the nations, are supporting this duck-faced scheme. I think myself there might be something to it. A universal government supported by a mighty military force and engaged in coercion at the top level, supported by the people below. It's unheard of, yet it seems to be happening, and soon, too. What's really scary, though, is what's happened to human rights. Timothie, I'm scared."

"I know. LGBT marriage and rights are threatened on all sides in Europe and the States. How long before the KKK come to Canada? Gay marriage will be a thing of the past."

"On a brighter note, every nation seems to be supporting free drugs."

"Free drugs? You mean pot?"

"No, really," Gianni's voice crackled over the Android. "It's really the opioid of the peoples. Christianity has gone viral, too, the bad kind. And Muslims are hiding. The Indians are very unpopular here in England.

Racism is everywhere, sexism, you name it, and all supported by the people and their governments. Especially the U.S., who is leading this."

"Maybe they're not," Timothie mused, rubbing his cheek with his hand. "Maybe it's being led by something or someone more sinister."

"Like what? Who's more sinister than Dennis Ducksworth, the President of the U.S.A.?"

"I think maybe you have it in your hand," Timothie replied.

"What? You're talking in riddles."

"I'll be there in four weeks. The first of March. And I'll pack light."

He would pack light, just his gym bag and Cloak of Power. Timothie hoped Uriel would accompany him because he'd need all the help he could get. The future of the world was at stake. Not in England, not in the States, not in Europe, Africa, or Asia, although the threat was worldwide. No, right here in Canada, in Edmonton, the threat was real and spreading.

He'd need time away to regroup and reconsider, and London, U.K. was perfect, where he could talk to someone he trusted and knew would be immune to the sinister forces of Prototype B. If Reginald were smart enough to put a cross into the game, as he may, the new craze would be a hit with the evangelicals as well, and that would put the frosting on the cupcake. My gosh, he was glad he wasn't from the Middle East! Though according to his friend, they were all playing the new game as well.

No one was safe in this brave new world. He gnawed on a finger. Perhaps there was something to be done, but Reginald would have to be roped into it.

Uriel, where are you?

Great white wings spread against the windows. Ah, that would do. An Angel and a superhero and the world to conquer!

Of course, Timothie was up to it. He smiled and dug into his gym bag. The cloak whipped out and around his broad shoulders, and he soared through the opaque windows into the arms of his Angel.

Chapter Thirteen

As though the altitude weren't cold enough, and the air rarified enough, Timothie flew on dangerous jets of air that whistled past polar flights, migrating birds, and military aircraft. He sliced over the Hudson Bay, part of Greenland, just missed Iceland, over the North Atlantic Ocean, and whirled into London, England.

Only four weeks ago he had accepted Gianni's invitation to visit him in London, with the aim of connecting with an old friend and sorting out the mystery of the Millennial Goggles. During that time, the game introduced by TopStrategy Marketing two months earlier had gone viral. Almost everyone was wearing the ubiquitous yellow goggles. Even the Prime Minister was filmed playing the game. The neuroscience contained in the frames made microchips obsolete.

Timothie had another lunch with Reginald after his talk with Gianni, but they were at cross purposes. He knew Reginald to be a good man at heart, but he had been corrupted by his love of power and money, and his chance to attain absolute control over a segment of the world that gleefully acquiesced. Timothie looked around him and saw zombies created by a mass hallucination.

As arranged, Gianni met him in Covent Garden on the eastern fringes of the West End in Soho. Timothie's cape and a change of clothing were stowed in his black leather backpack. He wore his white Jaws movie poster tee-shirt with a splash of red, white Diesel low-rise jeans, and a white Converse baseball hat. Gianni was obviously influenced by British fashion, in a black turtleneck and black jeans with Nike runners. They embraced.

"Timothie, I'm so glad to see you!"

"I thought you were in Rome!"

"No, I'm in the U.K. again for the short term anyhow. Always wanted to show you around Soho and my neighborhood here. Are you hungry, man? The pub food is excellent. Here, let's pop into the Pig & Cross and have a genuine Irish beer and some bangers and mash. Or something more continental, if you please. Got British money?"

"Well, yes, I changed some before I got here, old man. Diet Pepsi will do for me, and a plowman's lunch is fine. Had that at the Druid in Edmonton."

Gianni laughed and slapped his old friend on the back. "Oh, come on, you can do better than that!" The labyrinthine Pig & Cross was only a short walk away, full of nooks and crannies, and Timothie smiled his crooked grin with delight on the way into the polished wood and leather interior.

Over a mezze platter with Mediterranean favorites, they chatted about old times, about their lives now, and about their future plans.

"What's this about our old friend, Reginald Smith?" Gianni asked. "He's responsible for the Millennial Goggles? That's what they're calling them now, though the box says Prototype B. Not catchy at all. Not at all for a catchy new game."

"I'm afraid it's more than a game," Timothie said. "You wouldn't believe me if I told you."

"Try me."

Timothie considered, sitting on the other side of the table, his fingers laced like a steeple. He began by outlining Reginald's success, his inheritance and the Lamborghini in the underground parking lot under the prestigious Oyster penthouse apartment Reginald bought with his deceased relative's estate, the job he kept at TopStrategy Marketing, and the success of his new project, which really wasn't Reginald's project at all, but something stolen from the gates of Hell. Timothie cleared his throat and glanced at his friend. Gianni was listening intently, slim face bowed over his plate of hummus and pita.

"I believe you," he murmured. "I know Reginald from old times. He was always interested in the dark side of things. When he wasn't smoking pot he was conjuring from old books, but as far as I know, it never got him anywhere. Now you say he's hooked on something bigger than he can handle?"

"Yes, I think so," Timothie said. "This new game, it changes people's perceptions. My assistants can't think of anything else, and they're suddenly very passive and open to all kinds of conspiracy theories. It's like they've lost their ability to think for themselves."

Gianni looked around the pub. More than ninety percent of the customers wore the yellow goggles, immersed in their own thoughts, some giggling and others with expressions of awe on their faces. The dark red lenses burned and flashed. "Oh, and why doesn't it affect us in the same way?"

"I refused to wear the goggles for more than a few seconds. I could feel the pull of the game, though, simple though it seems. I took them off right away. Because I know what neuromarketing is, the way it affects the unconscious mind rather than the conscious mind, and affects our memories, too. This is something more sinister than that, even, Gianni. These glasses are like implants right into our souls. I don't know why you are unaffected."

"I've noticed that maybe one percent of the population isn't affected, old man."

"That's good news. We just have to find out why," Timothie mused.

"So, what or who are they responding to? If they're becoming zombies, who's their master?"

"I don't know. That's what I want to find out. It could be something even more sinister than Ducksworth and his minions. I mean really demonic. Not of this world."

"Ouch. Yeah, I see what you mean." Gianni toyed with his own Millennial Goggles, the yellow arms twisting in his smooth hands. "Something's been added to the images."

"What's that?"

"A cross. Crosses. Fiery and red."

Timothie flexed his strong biceps. "And pyramids?"

"That too," Gianni said. "It's a symbol now. It's more powerful than before. We didn't have to take the glasses back. They're controlling them from there."

"From where?"

"Why, wherever the power is coming from."

"Power, yes." *Bael.* Suddenly, Timothie didn't feel so hungry anymore. He pushed back his plate and got to his feet. "Let's go," he said. "I'd like to see London."

"Sure. We can take a double-decker bus to the rest of downtown. Maybe poke around a bookshop, book a tour to Big Ben and the Elizabeth Towers in the Parliament Buildings in Westminster, you can't miss that. Ride the Eye. England swings like a pendulum-doo, you know." He chuckled. "How long you here for?"

"A few days. I took some time off the salon. Got someone to fill in while I'm gone."

Gianni laughed again. "Not Reginald?"

"No, of course not. Young fellow used to work for the barber in the same space. Just for a few days. Paula and Skye are keeping an eye on him."

"Good idea. Now let's book that tour." His old friend popped out a Samsung Galaxy S8 and his fingers flew over the keyboard. "This afternoon all right?"

"Fine. Great."

* * *

The tour bus was full, and they had to climb up to the second deck. Timothie sat in the aisle seat, and Gianni cranked down the window, leaned out of the window while the bus lurched and careened toward Westminster. He whipped out his mobile. "I'll take some pics for you. We'll go out for Indian food later. But here, there's theatres and bookstores and high-end clothing shops, look, there's the entrance to the Tube where we could take the #9 to Harrod's. And look at the fashions on the street. Bet you don't see this in Edmonton." The tour director at the front of the bus expounded on the history of Westminster and the towers. Timothie yawned.

Gianni leaned further out the window just as the bus hit a pothole and lurched violently to one side, flinging Gianni partway out the upper deck. He hung onto the window frame, his phone clattering to the ground. Timothie, alarmed, grabbed his friend's leg as he swung out of his seat and clung to the side of the bus, screaming. His left knee was jammed into the frame and blood began to soak into his black jeans.

Timothie had no choice. Quickly, he wedged himself through the opening in the window, past Gianni's body, and held up the side of the double-decker bus as he simultaneously flung his friend's body back into his seat. It was done in an instant. He could see the great white beating wings of the Angel of the West over the front of the vehicle, guiding it, placing it firmly on the pavement, and then it was over. Timothie settled again into his seat beside his friend. The tour director droned on.

"How'd you *do* that, dude?" gasped Gianni, holding his leg with one hand while blood oozed past his white fingers.

A few of the nearby passengers gaped, but others wore their yellow goggles and were oblivious to the small drama that had just played out in front of them.

"Don't mention it," Timothie muttered. "It doesn't matter. Here, let me look at your leg." He touched it and the bleeding stopped. "I think you'll be okay."

Gianni gazed at his friend, his mouth open and his eyes wide. His eyebrows scraped the middle of his forehead. "No, I mean, you *flew*, dude. How'd you do that? What's going on? Is it something like you were talking about Reginald is up to, is that what it is? You're suddenly superman?"

"No, really."

A small boy tapped Timothie on the shoulder. "How'd you do that, mister?" the child asked. "Are you Spiderman? Where's your cape?"

"It's in the bag," muttered Timothie and winked. "Uriel! Help."

"Who's Uriel?" Gianni looked with astonishment at his hand where his mobile gleamed. "I'm sure I dropped this," he said. "What's going on? This is really spooky. It's really sort of scary, old man."

Huge white wings covered the bus as it careened past Westminster Abbey, and everyone on the bus except Timothie closed their eyes for only a few seconds – less than a minute, mind you – and when they opened their eyes, they had forgotten.

"Look at these pics," Gianni muttered. "Aren't they something? And look – we're here already! Where's the time gone?"

"Indeed," Timothie replied. "Why," he said, as the tour director droned on, "I do think we're here. With no harm done, right, kid?"

"Right, mister." The small boy frowned then went back to sharing his sweeties with his grandmother. "That's Big Ben right there. You new to London, mister?"

"Yes," Timothie said. *New here. New to the planet. New to the people. Lonely for my home.* No amount of travel could take away the homesickness he felt for Draxxt and his people. Today he'd made a mistake and almost been found out. *Thanks, Uriel,* he breathed.

"You're my child," breathed a great warm voice from all around him, and he settled comfortably into his seat just as the bus stopped. He swayed. The passengers began to disembark at the base of the famous clock tower.

"We'll see Buckingham Palace day after tomorrow, that okay?" asked his friend, snapping pictures. Timothie took a dozen selfies in front of the tower.

"Yes," he said. "No problems."

Chapter Fourteen

Timothie and Gianni talked far into the night. Gianni's clock struck one and then two. A little ball of fur purred on Gianni's lap – his kitten Maxx. The flat was cool and postmodern, with many souvenirs of Rome and other locales dotted around the rooms. Gianni sipped wine, and Timothie sipped coffee, and the night ticked by. At first, the conversation centered on Maude.

"I feel sad that she was sick," Timothie shared. "I saw her weak and vulnerable leaning against that old car, throwing up into the street. I know it wasn't her in my shop, and that Bael left her out on the street feeling sick. He can take any form he chooses. Reginald deserves it, but Maude does not."

"She's a witch, you say?" Gianni asked. "She'll be okay. She can protect herself."

"Against a demon?

"So you say, old chap. I knew someone once who felt sorry for demons. They know they've lost."

Timothie chewed on his third oatmeal cookie. "Bael doesn't know that. He wants to usurp the throne of God himself."

"Who told you that?"

Timothie went silent, chewing, slurped on his coffee, and traced wet circles on the oilcloth with his finger.

"It was Reginald, wasn't it? Because Reginald and the truth were never well acquainted."

"You never did like him," Timothie observed, biting into a red apple.

"For good reason, it would appear. What did Maude do wrong, that she should be a target?" Gianni swirled the burgundy liquid in his cup. "I really should get some proper red wine glasses," he said. "These are for sherry."

"Darling, you're so particular."

"All I want is a little of the good life. What about Maude? Don't you think she can take care of herself? I've never met the lady, but I think from what you say that she could come up with some sort of spell that's powerful."

"She needs something to protect herself, and she was there in the Grand Canyon and helped with the cleansing of the Colorado River when Crazy Jack polluted it. She *is* powerful, in her way."

"Sounds to me as though Bael has been busy."

Timothie considered. He tipped the chrome coffee pot and half a cup of dark steaming liquid spilled into his yellow and white china cup. "I never thought of that at the time. Could be, but the Dareboy has his own demons and has been known to create a lot of trouble when he's around. I knew him on Draxxt, you know."

"Draxxt? Ah, yes. That mythical planet you talk about so infrequently," Gianni murmured and yawned. He stretched both long arms over his head, and his chair scraped against the table as he stood up. Timothie slouched in his seat.

"Are you comfortable in the spare room?" Gianni asked. "I'm going to turn in now."

"We haven't decided anything and tomorrow's my last day here," Timothie objected. "What do I do about Reginald? Is he really doomed, and should I send him down the drain with his demon? He was once a friend. The cray-cray old woman, Maude, what about her?"

"We're all responsible for our own actions," Gianni said, leaning against the table. "You know that. So do Reginald and Maude. You don't have to fix them. You don't have to save the world." A pair of yellow goggles lay on the table beside the empty wine bottle. Gianni picked them up and popped them onto his nose. The kitten jumped from his lap and skittered across the carpet to a bowl of milk in the corner. It began to lap the milk. "I can see the psychedelic colors. I can feel the pull on my brain. But it's up to me to pull the plug. Nobody takes over the world without consent, my friend."

Timothie squirmed. "You don't believe me."

Gianni sighed. "Sure, I believe you. We've been together for five days and four nights since you appeared in Coventry Garden to meet me. Amongst the tents, buskers, orators, and street performers, you seemed quite normal to me, Tim." He laughed. "We've talked into the night since you arrived, and I know your life very well, and though I can't remember falling out of a double-decker bus on the way to Big Ben, you say I did, and I do remember a lapse of time when anything could have happened. I know when I met you years ago, when we were both cray-cray teenagers, you had a wild story that I half-believed. I believe that you have a guardian Angel and that together you are going to save the world. But forgive me, old friend, if I remain skeptical about your chances."

"Is it my chances or my story you don't believe?" asked Timothie. Springing into the spare bedroom, he emerged with the silver-spangled cloak over his shoulders. *Uriel,* he breathed, and the Angel responded as always with a feathery embrace. Timothie levitated six inches off the carpet, spread his arms, and *flew*. He darted from one corner of the room to the other, up, down, and sideways, swooshing past his friend in a flurry of flapping velvet ebony and stars. Uriel appeared. Heavenly laughter shook the room.

"Holy shit!" exclaimed Gianni. "Yes, I believe you now, Tim, but I'm not sure I believe my own eyes. You've kept this a secret all these years?"

"No secret," Timothie swooshed past his friend like a black bolt of lightning, then alighted on navy Converse runners in front of the leather couch, where he threw himself onto the pillows. His white and navy Adidas cap skewed at a crazy angle. His muscles bulged out of the sleeveless denim vest he wore, and chest hairs swirled about a silver cross around his neck. Tall, snowy, and beautiful, Uriel clapped her great hands and disappeared.

"That show was for me?" asked Gianni, putting his fists together. "I believe you can change the world. You have power and justice on your side. The power of good, if that Angel is to be believed and isn't a product of the wine."

"This is real," Timothie assured him. "It's why I flew to London to see you, Gianni. Now can we talk?"

"Yes. For sure."

"I can save the world. We're going to do it."

"We?" Gianni scuttled into the kitchen to make another pot of coffee. "I'm going to need this," he mused, pouring extra grounds into the basket.

"I and my good friends," finished Timothie, unclasping the cloak from his neck. "It's too big for me. I know enough to ask for help."

"No. No, you don't have to," objected Gianni. "You have the power. All you need is confidence."

"Is that what I flew across the ocean to hear?" The little ball of fur put its black and white paws on the side of the sofa. "Jump," Timothie said, laughing at its antics. The kitten tried twice, and on the third time, it succeeded.

"You're new to power. You've always felt, rather, powerless. You don't know what you possess at your fingertips."

Timothie shook his head. "I need Reginald on my side. I need Maude, you, and Crazy Jack Dareboy."

"Maybe you do if it gives you confidence. Ultimately, you're alone. We're all alone. Little flecks of body tissue, water, and blood scattered over the surface of a beating heart. A soul covered in Gucci garments. What is the demon but one raw soul stripped to its grasping desires and nothing else human or angelic remains of it? You're a hero. We're all heroes. Time we acted like it." He threw the yellow goggles from his nose. Sparks and hissing sounds crackled across the small expanse of the oilcloth.

"It's angry," Timothie said. "I can feel it. I can hear it, Gianni."

"On your way home tomorrow, think about me and the freedom I have, pal."

"Freedom. Yes. So important. Now that you know about the Cloak of Power, I can tell you my Angel and the cloak make me free."

"You've always been free, Timothie. You are a free spirit. Minimalist, free thinker, drama llama. Ha."

"You're right there, Gianni," Timothie replied and smirked. He threw his cape back into the backpack and began to prepare for bed. Tomorrow was a long trip over the Atlantic, and he would have to avoid Iceland again if he could – the fumes from Hekla warned him that an eruption could follow him home and the ashes could affect his friend in London as they had in 2010. Perhaps more so, scientists monitoring the volcano warned of an impending catastrophe. *So much anxiety.*

"I don't think you have to worry. We've had crises before and we'll have them again. Dennis Ducksworth is only one of many world leaders to be a few pickles short of a sandwich. You don't have to worry about Reginald, either. He's always been a troublemaker and an oddball. We both know that God is bigger than any demon. So, what's to worry about?"

"I love you, Gianni," Timothie said and hugged his friend. Maxx peered up at them with huge golden eyes. The cat began to purr. Timothie leaned down and stroked the little ball of fur under its chin. It hissed at him and swatted. He laughed. "The cat is all yours," he said. "Let's go to bed now. We can talk more in the morning, but I want an early start."

"I want you to be safe, my friend," Gianni replied, scooping up the tuxedo kitten in his manly arms.

"I want the world to be safe." Timothie frowned, his deep brown eyes thoughtful.

"And it will be. We're secure in the arms of a loving universe. Not a predictable universe, but a trustworthy one."

"I hope you're right," Timothie said. The cape stirred in its place and outside the wide windows, a flurry of white pinions brushed against the sky.

Chapter Fifteen

Untouched by the cauldron that was Iceland's future, Timothie flew the next day over the Atlantic Ocean, retraced his route to Edmonton and touched down outside his digs on Ada Boulevard. A new resolve pushed him up the stairs to his third level apartment facing the river valley. He more or less collapsed on his cognac leather couch in the living room, pushed a yellow and orange cushion under his neck, and closed his eyes for a moment. It had been a long trip. His rooms faced south, but remnants of orange and gold stretched around the purple skyline of the city near the southwest. He never tired of the view. Fatigued but satisfied with the outcome of his trip and the positive conversation last night, Timothie plotted the next stage of his adventure.

Maude. Did Bael's possession leave her weak and sickly, vulnerable to another demonic attack? Timothie's heart warmed when he thought of his elderly client and friend who had followed him from Draxxt. The couch yielded to his weight, and the cushion was soft and cool. He drifted into a fitful sleep, a muscular arm thrown over his eyes.

* * *

Several bookings later at the salon the next day, the superhero paused in the midst of a shampoo, head cocked to one side, listening. Only recently he'd discovered acute hearing skills to match his radiographic vision when he was in the right mode of attention. Like a lion with his pride, he led Pauline and Skye from the back spas to the front door, his client immersed in purple suds at the sink.

"What is it?" whispered Skye, her pink and white scrubs spotless in the streaming noon sun which dappled the lobby.

"You'll have to trust me," Timothie said. "Lock the doors."

"Where are you?" complained his client.

"Right here, dear. I'm keeping you safe."

Mrs. Dunlop sputtered. "Safe? What's happening in here?"

"Nothing at all out of the way, darling. I heard something. Skye and Pauline heard it, too. Did you hear anything?"

"No, certainly not. Now get back here and finish my hair!"

"Of course. I never leave a client. I take good care of my ladies. Just want to make sure the salon is secure."

"I don't know why it wouldn't be," Mrs. Dunlop said. "You're a strong fellow, and the girls can look after themselves. It's not a bad area. Wait! I do hear something. Like a scream."

Timothie locked the doors and closed the blinds. "Yes, that's what I detected, too. It's coming this way."

He continued with the shampoo, rinsed her silver hair, and wrapped a thick white towel around her head. A banshee screeched just outside the windows.

Suddenly, he heard Maude's old car roaring down the street to come to a halt outside the salon. "I'd know the sound of that Benz anywhere," he said and smiled. He led Mrs. Dunlop to the silver chair, where she peered into the mirror as he began to snip the ends off her curls. The banshee wailed, a wind whipped his sign outside to clatter in the street, and the door of Maude's old car banged shut.

"I'm here!" he heard his old friend shout, and sure enough, it was Maude the witch who swirled around the remnants of his sign outside, lifted up the billboard with one muscular old hand, smashed it back into place on the sidewalk, and strode to the locked door. Every inch of her ash blonde hair was perfect, like a halo surrounding a fierce and antagonistic visage. "I'm here and so is the devil himself, and I'm damned if I'll let him in!"

"We'll keep him out," agreed Timothie, and Mrs. Dunlop stared at her reflection in the hanging mirror. She smiled slightly as her silver curls bobbed into place.

Timothie swished away the towel around her shoulders and shook it. "Come with me, luv, and sit under the dryer for twenty minutes." She followed him as Maude appeared inside the doors, blue eyes flashing like lightsabers and charms dribbling through her fingers. She dropped her large old red and white Coach bag onto the table by the windows and threw open the blinds.

"You won't frighten Maude McKenna," she cried to the shade hovering outside the windows, slavering at the glass. Large droplets of slime ran down the panes, and the demon screamed again. Maude's stolid figure stood between Mrs. Dunlop and the demon. Timothie put one sinewy hand on her shoulder.

"No need to protect me," he said. "I have the Cloak of Power and Uriel nearby."

"You don't need no Angel to protect you nor a cloak of midnight stars, my boy. All you need is the witch of Draxxt. This demon from Hell took me over unawares last time I was here, and it won't do it again." She flung her arms to the ceiling. Rainbow-colored charms cascaded from her white, wrinkled hands. The demon roared, and slimy tentacles inched between the panes onto the hardwood floors, which were stained with the demon's blood. Skye advanced with a curling iron in her hand, and Paula behind her brandished a large mirror. Mrs. Dunlop sat beneath the dryer. She hummed and leafed through a fashion magazine, oblivious to the drama.

"My cloak!" Timothie cried. "I left it at home!"

"No matter, it's not the cloak, it's the belief that's powerful," Maude said. The windows creaked with the force of the gale outside, the sign rattled in the street, vehicles purred by and occasional passersby hurried along 118 Avenue, huddled in their spring clothes because after all, it was

March and not supposed to be this cold. The temperature had dropped precipitously by about twenty degrees Celsius. Ice formed outside. The demon howled, and parts of it squirmed onto the floor, dripping green blood. Timothie, helpless without his cape, stood by and called for Uriel. No Angel appeared.

"Where is he?" The superhero was stripped of his powers. Maude stood tall between him and the raging demon. She screeched incantations, which swirled on the wind that whirled into the rooms and out again through the broken glass.

Bael reared back. Its face flamed, and its mouth was cavernous; its talons ripped at Maude's arms. Timothie strode to her side and threw his bulging biceps and strong arms in front of his friend.

"I may not have my cloak. I may not have my Angel. But, by God, I know that good overcomes evil, and that is what's going to happen, Maude, my friend. We did more than this on the new planet when the Trolls usurped our lands and the fairies cast their spells, where the Picts strode on many leagued boots. My liege the King taught me to fight, and he didn't use magic; he used skill and the art of swordsmanship. So shall I today." He drew a long pair of golden shears from a drawer and slashed at the demon's questing dripping fingers.

Bael screamed as Timothie slashed its hand from its arm. The demon waved the stump, which spurted green blood onto Timothie's dress shirt with the sleeves cut off, and the low-rise jeans, and the white Converse sneakers. All were covered in green slime. Timothie slashed again, and Maude screamed incantations. Mrs. Dunlop turned a page, oblivious to the scene. Paula and Skye danced and swirled, fencing with their curling iron and mirror. The stereo crashed as Jann Arden sang "Living Under June." The gale roared into the room, scattering papers, and a jar of combs tipped over.

"What's up, man?" Crazy Jack Dareboy skipped through the locked doors. He confronted Paula and Skye, ushered them gently back to their spas, filled the Bodum with boiling water, and made a pot of coffee. Bael snarled and slashed. Crazy Jack slurped his steaming mug of coffee, peering at the demon over the rim of his cup. "What's this? Competition?" he asked. "Where's the creamer?"

Timothie danced in front of Maude, slashing at Bael with the shears. "Cross yourself!" Maude yelled. "This next one is a good one." She stood like a white cracked statue near the shards of glass and the dripping twelve-foot demon. Timothie dropped the shears and made the sign of the cross as best he remembered from a Catholic friend.

Maude scattered a few herbs in a jar and lit them with a lighter she drew from her bra. She grew in stature until she stood toe to toe with the fearsome slathering enemy. "*In the name of the Eternal Lady and Lord, I bid thee part. I consecrate and clear this space. Let nothing but joy linger here.*"

Bael laughed. Crazy Jack sauntered to the front of the salon. He crossed himself, drew a silver blade from his belt, and plunged it into Bael's still beating heart. As though he sat down to a light lunch with a friend, Crazy Jack settled himself onto the window ledge and began to twist the dagger. Bael screamed. Timothie grasped the shears once again and made them into a golden cross, blinding Bael with a light that suddenly shot from the icon into the demon's red and black eyes.

"I'm not finished yet," roared Bael, striking out blindly. As he did so, a rush of wings and a gentle breeze entered the room while a soft feminine voice enveloped the trio in peace.

"I am here," Uriel whispered. The demon was crushed beneath a ton of white feathers and a nova of light. Like a freight train, a tornado screamed into the room, carrying away the demon and the Angel together. The shattered glass spun together in the rushing air currents, the temperature bloomed to a sunny thirty degrees, and the window reappeared once again intact. Mrs. Dunlop looked up and turned off the dryer with her wrinkled old fingers.

"I think I'm done," she quavered. "Henry will be here soon to collect me. Time for my blow-out, Timothie."

Dareboy sheathed his long silver blade. He sipped on the cup of coffee still in his left hand. He hadn't spilled a drop. "Crazy," was all he said.

Timothie shook his head, smiled his crooked smile, and embraced Maude and Dareboy with a huge bearhug.

"I'm so glad you're my friends," he said. "Thank you. Thank you."

Dareboy sat with a thump on the chair in the corner. A piece of ivy trailed over his boot. Maude collapsed next to him, panting.

"Timothie?" asked Mrs. Dunlop.

"Coming, dear," was all he could say. He stood behind the silver chair as she settled herself.

"Where's Reginald?" Dareboy slouched in his chair. "He's the only one missing."

"I suspect he's busy with *these*." Timothie picked up a pair of yellow goggles that Skye had left behind. "He has a world to conquer."

"And we have a world to save," smirked Dareboy.

Maude smiled. "You can't keep us down," she said. "I am a woman who runs with the wolves."

Timothie glanced out the windows. He saw a flash of wings that hovered over Maude's Benz. "You are indeed."

"It's not over yet." Dareboy twirled his little black mustache with a dark finger and ran a hand through his dreadlocks. "We've only just begun." He popped a pair of yellow goggles over his eyes. "I think I'm a zombie. It's happening, Timothie. Help me!"

"You're incorrigible," Timothie said, helping Mrs. Dunlop from her chair. Henry Dunlop rattled the front door knob. "Oops, forgot. It's locked." He strode through the lobby and greeted Henry.

"Hi, Timothie. You ready?" Henry asked his wife. He patted his rotund belly. Mrs. Dunlop simpered.

"Yes, Henry."

"Anything exciting happen while I was gone?" Henry asked. Mrs. Dunlop took his arm, her freshly permed hair shining in the afternoon sun.

"Nothing out of the way happened today," she said. "Just an ordinary day."

Dareboy doubled over laughing. Henry glanced at him suspiciously.

Timothie offered Henry a cup of coffee. “No, thank you,” he said. “Too late in the day for caffeine, you know. I wouldn’t sleep.”

“I might have trouble sleeping myself, tonight,” Timothie murmured, cracking open a can of diet Pepsi.

“Be careful with all that caffeine,” Henry warned. “It’ll kill you.”

Chapter Sixteen

Afterward, chatting in a somewhat desultory fashion together and over their phones, Skye and Paula, as well as many of Timothie's friends and clients, increasingly voiced concern for his mental wellbeing. "A party!" enthused Paula, in her pink smock and lavender pants. "Yes! We can gather his favorite people together and maybe figure out where to go from here, or at least – at least – show him that we love and support him."

Details were rapidly sketched together. A few days later, Timothie's salon served as the setting for an impromptu soiree. Timothie, fresh from a run outside, was surprised, on entering the salon, by many old friends he hadn't seen for several years, including Reginald's parents, some favorite clients, and a beloved former teacher. They believed a party was much needed to lighten the mood of what had become a sinister and convoluted conspiracy plot; some felt it was in Timothie's own mind, but most were beginning to believe him. They had seen the magic of what he could do, and Bael's appearance at Jane's Texas Steakhouse changed for those present the incongruity of Timothie's beliefs. There was talk of devil worship, and Reginald's absence at this party was all the more suspect.

"I wasn't planning on a party, but this is great," Timothie said, his eyebrows rising. "There's a bottle of wine in the back, and I'll bring out some snacks. I drink wine, but not very often. I think tonight I'll have the vintage diet Pepsi."

"I locked the doors," Paula said as she leaned on the stereo console. "Skye, can you bring the crackers and cheese?"

Skye skittered into the back kitchen and emerged with a couple of plates of crackers, cheese, and pepperoni scavenged from the refrigerator. Dareboy hugged his host and took the bottle of red wine into his slim fingers. He poured half a glass of wine for Timothie's former junior high school teacher, who settled into an armchair and sipped, his ginger hair and minimal goatee flaming under the lights. "We went to school together," the teacher smirked, and Timothie laughed. "Yes, as student and teacher," he said. "I'm much younger, of course!"

The former teacher gazed with wide innocent eyes at Reginald's father, also a retired educator. "He robbed the cradle," he commented.

"You two will have a lot to talk about, both retired teachers," Reginald's mother said and left the teachers to talk about special needs students and their challenges. Dareboy threw his arm around the former teacher and winked at Timothie.

"We're all here to support you, man," Dareboy said. "Things have gotten a little rough lately, and we want you to know you're not alone."

"Did you two know about this?" asked Timothie of his assistants.

"They planned it," laughed Dareboy.

Both Skye and Paula moved through the room, chatting, patting shoulders, and passing out snacks. A very tall, slim fellow and his partner stood in a corner away from the general crowd. Maude took both of them in hand; squeezed their shoulders, brought them drinks, and even Henry and Mrs. Dunlop showed up. A tall man in a cowboy hat attended with his entrepreneurial wife. A striking woman in a red dress and bling winked at Timothie, and her husband gave the entrepreneur a high five.

Crazy Jack Dareboy dressed normally for a change, out of his red jumpsuit, in blue jeans, white Converse runners, and a khaki jacket. "Hey, Timothie," he called from his perch on the back of the teacher's chair. "Want me to get more snacks or some beer? There's a liquor store just down the street, and I can stop for snacks on the way there. Will only take a minute."

Timothie moved around the room. He beamed at his friends. "I didn't know I had so many good friends. What a surprise. Thank you all for coming."

Mrs. Dunlop twittered on the arm of her stalwart husband. "That nice boy phoned us all and let us know you're in need of some support from your buddies, Timothie. Of course, Henry and I are glad to come. But I don't know what's wrong. Everything seemed fine last time I was here. Did you hear about the stabbing, though? Just a few blocks away from your salon. Happened day before yesterday."

"No," Timothie said. He stopped to pour Cowboy Hat a glass of wine. "And yes, Dareboy, we could use some diet Pepsis and maybe some imported beers. And some ice. A couple bottles of red wine. I'll set up a bucket of ice in the lobby."

"All taken care of, man." Dareboy bounded through the room on rubber soles and almost flew out the door. The tall, slim man in the corner left his partner, who was coughing, and accompanied Crazy Jack. "We'll take my car," he said. "It's that blue Ford Escape out there around the corner. Bill's not feeling quite up to snuff tonight. I'll drive."

"I can see it," Jack called.

"He can see around corners," Timothie laughed. It was true.

Twenty minutes later, the room filled with chatter, bright faces, and good food and drink. Timothie beamed at his friends and lifted his vintage green glass bottle of diet Pepsi to toast Reginald's father, who lounged in a silver chair in front of the mirror and told interesting stories of Reginald's youth, including Timothie's more recent history. "Don't, Mr. Smith," he said and chuckled. The father smiled.

"Reg sure looks like his dad," Maude commented. "Same eyes, same smile."

"The apple didn't fall far from the tree," Reginald's mother said. "Same mustache." She squeezed her husband's shoulder.

Timothie's eyes sparkled as he gazed at the older man. "My hero. Next to my own father, you are my hero. I don't know how you produced such a son, though, dear." The father grunted and shifted in his chair.

"That could be taken both ways. My son is a good man. Gone a little bad, I admit."

Back from the store, Dareboy and his tall friend passed out beers, diet Cokes, and Nanaimo bars. A grey-haired woman with a pleasant face tied the front of her plaid shirt together around her waist and commented on how good the cheese spread tasted. The teacher poured more wine. Timothie, for a change, was lost for words as he gazed around the room at his good friends who had come together to offer support. He did notice that several of them had brought yellow goggles, but all laid them on the stereo cabinet or a table.

Timothie clapped his hands. Intent on their conversations, no one stopped talking, so he took a dinner knife from the serving platter and banged it on a wine glass. His friends stopped their chatting and looked in his direction. "Thank you," he said. "I want your attention for just a moment. It's about the yellow goggles, the Millennial Goggles. I want your opinion. Do you notice any change after wearing them?"

"My son thinks they're the coolest thing," Plaid Shirt said. "His friends and he all get together at parties and do nothing but play the game. It's very addictive, he said."

"How about you?" asked Timothie. "Do you think it affects your willpower or your thinking in any way? Any different from how you usually think?"

Reginald's father objected. "I've never tried them, but Reg has."

"What does he think?"

"He has changed, come to think of it. Now that you mention it, Timothie. He seems more preoccupied, more observant to the sort of politics that are going over now on the internet, he says. He has been affected, I think. The manufacturers say they're going to put out an enhancement next week, too. They didn't say what, but they don't need the glasses back. It'll be immediately updated by some sort of software that's in the frames. Why, I even think that Reg had something to do with their manufacture. He's a clever man. But the politics seem beyond him. I must say, I know he has something to do with that company of his and the goggles, maybe something not good. He has changed. Yes. Not for the better. I don't know if the goggles or his workload have anything to do with it. But others? Yes, Tim. This new game has changed the country. I'm concerned."

Dareboy pursed his lips. "We were afraid of that. It's only the first step in a total takeover."

A cacophony of voices interrupted. "What do you mean?"

"What takeover?"

"Is this some kind of conspiracy theory?"

Timothie held up a hand to silence them. "TopStrategy Marketing put these out only six weeks ago, and already they've gone viral. It won't be long until everyone in every household is wearing them and playing the new game. There'll be updates to it. If you must wear them and play the game, please be careful, and let Jack and I know how they affect you. We have reason to believe that TopStrategy is not only trying to take over the market on new software but on people's souls as well."

"What?" Nervous laughter permeated the room.

"We're here to support you, Tim," said the general consensus, sparked by Reginald's father. "But this sounds like a conspiracy theory. I know you've had a lot of trouble with old friends in your life, and there've been some odd goings on around the salon that can't be explained. But this, taking over people's souls, that's a bit much, don't you think? Nobody can do that, and we all know that..."

"...God is in control!" finished Reginald's mother, squeezing her husband's shoulder.

"Yes," Timothie agreed. Nearby, Dareboy pinched his lip and stood, legs wide apart, at the window looking out. "God is in control. But there's a dark side, too. Thank you all so much for being here. I really need the support. I'm fighting the dark side, and it's real, it's not something in me that needs to be fought, it's an outside force, and Jack and I have seen it."

"So have we," agreed Skye and Paula. They nodded.

"What does it have to do with the new game and the goggles?" asked the tall man's quiet partner, who coughed in his corner of the room.

He sat in one of the silver chairs. "We love the new game. It keeps us occupied for hours and away from the TV. I think it's a good thing. My mind feels refreshed after I've played it. Then I play it some more and – you're right, there's something that takes over. But in the first place, it feels like a bolt of energy to a tired brain." He coughed again. "I've come down with something. Excuse me." His partner patted his shoulder.

"What does it feel like after you've played it all night?" Timothie asked. Paula twisted her pair of yellow goggles in her hands and finally put them on. She smiled with apparent delight.

"Like I would do anything to keep on playing. I don't know what the upgrade will be, but I've heard there's some religious images on it, and the game will go to a new level, where our minds will control more than the shapes and colors. We have to change our thinking and make a quantum leap. It will be so exciting."

"Exciting, yes," Timothie mused, swirling the bottle of soda in his hand. "I don't drink a lot, but I know how to recognize when someone has had too much to drink. And I don't play this game, but I know how to recognize when it's getting dangerous."

"Oh, no," they all chorused. "It's a fun game! Why, everyone's doing it."

The teacher played with his wine glass as he slouched in the armchair. "Seriously, Timothie. If you're concerned, I think we all should be concerned. But what can a roomful of people do? This game is worldwide."

"It's gone viral," agreed Cowboy Hat's wife.

"We have to do something," Timothie said. "And I know how."

Dareboy smirked. He slapped the window glass with his right hand and held a beer with his other. "We know who's behind it," he explained. "We know how to get to him, and we know his power."

"Yes," Timothie mused. "We know his power."

"That's the problem," Dareboy said. He levitated two inches off the floor. No one appeared to notice. Timothie motioned to him, and his shoes touched the floor again. "It's far beyond human."

"That's what I was afraid you were going to say," his former teacher said. "I need to be convinced."

"His name is Reginald Smith, and I've invited his parents here so maybe they can talk to him, too. Reg's mom and dad are like my own to me."

He continued, "He's the Director of Marketing at TopStrategy Marketing. He got that way because he has brains, money, and connections. Especially connections. He's not evil himself, but he's got himself mixed up in some seriously bad stuff."

The teacher frowned. "Like the Mafia or motorcycle gangs?"

"Worse than that."

"What could be worse than that?" asked Reginald's mother.

Dareboy levitated over to Timothie, and they put their arms around each other's shoulders. Dareboy ruffled Timothie's hair. "Hell itself," he said. There was a gasp from the room.

"I always said it was the end times," someone commented.

Suddenly, the room was filled with noise like a freight train thundered through. Lightning flashed in a corner. Timothie ran to the counter where his gym bag was stored and threw on the Cloak of Power. The cloak billowed out and covered some of his friends who stood nearby.

"We'll protect you," he cried. Dareboy tossed out his arms, and great shards of light sizzled from his fingers. The noise of the freight train diminished into the distance. The top popped from a bottle of wine. A glass shattered. Night closed in outside the windows. Dareboy closed the blinds, and the woman in the striking red dress strode to the doors.

"They're locked," she said.

Timothie stood tall, so tall, then shot *through the windows* and above the salon, while Crazy Jack Dareboy held the noise and storm in the salon at bay and quiet with his outstretched arms.

"I can't believe it," gasped Reginald's mother. "If only his sister could see this now. She always said we're living at the end of days. This is proof if nothing else."

"Are we safe?" asked someone from the back.

"Yes, of course, so long as we're here and Timothie is wearing his Cloak of Power, we're safe. He wanted to warn you. Now he's warned you, and Bael and his people know you're aware."

"Are we in danger?" Reginald's father asked.

"No. The only danger is not knowing." Dareboy hovered well above the floorboards, his hands a lightning storm of power.

Timothie flew back in through the windows. "Nothing out there," he said. "False alarm. A minor demon or two, that's all."

"A demon?" Mrs. Dunlop screeched. "Oh, Henry!"

"That's all right, dear," Henry consoled her. "It's just a bad dream."

Timothie hovered in midair, his hands spread in a gesture of peace. "Now I have you all together and you all see this, and believe, I want to let you know that the evilness of end of days will never happen in your lifetimes. Evil will never take over the world, and there won't be any Revelations-type curse for the Earth, not so long as we can prevent it, and we can, with Divine help. God is in control. Good will overcome evil. The prophecies have been challenged, and we are not going to allow a thousand years of the Devil's rule, nor are the prophecies correct. Revelations was written to confuse the Romans and the Jews who would persecute the Christians. They have confused Christians themselves for too long. This may be the end times as prophesied. They seem to be, yes, I agree, but they will result in nothing less than glory if we fight hard against the black forces of evil."

"You have your army here," agreed his friends. "We'll all fight for you."

"No, you're fighting for your children and your children's children, and yourselves most of all, because this is going down right now."

"It can't be true!" wailed Mrs. Dunlop.

"It isn't true, darling," Henry consoled his wife. "It's just a bad dream. Come, let's go."

Timothie's sneakers hit the floor hard. "This is only the beginning. But we have allies you don't know of. The demon Bael wants to overcome the world and take his place on God's throne. That cannot be allowed."

"We won't allow it," his friends shouted and raised their glasses.

"It begins and ends with Reginald Smith."

"Death to Reginald!" screamed Timothie's supporters, not knowing what they said.

"No! He's a good man, misguided perhaps." His parents cried.

"No, not death, but rebirth," Timothie objected. "He's misguided, yes. He called up the demon Bael from his penthouse in the Oyster to give him power and even more money than he has because the love of money is the root of all evil."

"Not money itself," Mr. Smith commented.

"No," Timothie agreed. "Reginald is twisted, but he's not evil. I don't believe that of an old friend. We'll help to put him on the right path, and it's going to start here, tonight, with my friends and your knowledge of what the yellow glasses can do."

Paula swayed in a corner, still wearing her goggles, and giggled.

"It won't be easy," Skye commented. She tore the goggles from Paula's eyes. Paula drew back and screamed.

"Here," Dareboy said, "Have another glass of wine."

"Let's adjourn," called Maude. "There's more room in Jane's Texas Steakhouse tomorrow night, and does everyone remember Timothie's birthday?"

"No way!" they shouted.

"Yes! I'm bringing the cake and we'll have the whole thing catered there."

"Great idea! Happy birthday, Tim!"

"Nothing like an excuse for another party!" Timothie ducked his head and blushed. "I wasn't going to say anything. But it's my fiftieth tomorrow."

"Demons be blowed. This is something to celebrate," Reginald's father called from his perch on the side of the teacher's chair.

Timothie's Android trilled "Dixie."

"Timothie Hill speaking."

"Oh, hello, Reginald," he said. "We were just talking about you." He paused. "Yes, you're invited to a party tomorrow night."

Chapter Seventeen

Timothie leaned across the table at Jane's Texas Steakhouse as Reginald flipped a box of yellow goggles back and forth between his pale hands. The glasses rattled in the box. The red lenses flashed and sparked. At other tables nearby, no one engaged in conversation but they all possessed the power to cloud minds – a room of automatons. Reginald gestured at his fellow diners and grinned.

"Amazing, isn't it? Friggin' amazing," he said, adjusting a pair of goggles on his nose. "We tried to figure out how to bring them to life. It worked so well that even Dennis Ducksworth and Justin Harper wear them, and if you tune into the CBC or NBC news, then you'll see the effect on world policy."

"I noticed."

"Stephen Hawking has revised the doomsday clock one minute closer to total world oblivion. Fanatical religious cults stand on hillsides waiting for the end of the world. Look at our friends over there." Reginald gestured around the spacious dining room. "They're plugged into my propaganda. It's obedience first and reason second. People are suspending their disbelief."

Timothie's mouth dropped open. "Yes. It's worse than we thought. The brain isn't this perfectly rational organ. It has a very powerful, visceral effect on people's perceptions. But what are you plugging into their brains, Reginald? What do you and Bael hope to accomplish from this deception that has been placed on the world? My friends and I are the very few citizens I know who don't sit for hours in a trance as an example of addiction to this game. You say they're being fed information and propaganda from TopStrategy Marketing. What sort of information and what sort of propaganda are the citizens of this country expected to swallow? Before this, we've been fed by Hollywood, media, broadcasting, and internet."

"It was external. Now it's internal." Reginald smiled and smoothed his small blond mustache. "The reaction shakes one's faith in humanity's common sense and independence, doesn't it?"

"Yes. How can you do this, Reginald?"

"How? People are tired of listening to the latest crisis; they're concerned about democracy, they are anxious, scared, and angry. Many have found Nirvana in these goggles, in the Millennial Goggles, in Prototype B. They've emptied their minds and the whirling kaleidoscopic images they strive to control act very much like night goggles. Take the tiniest bit of light and amplify it enormously – converting the available photons into electrons, multiplying them, and then directing them at a light-emitting tube contained in the arms of the Millennial Goggles. Directly impacting the neurons of their brains, and then anything – *anything* – we tell them through those synapses will become embedded and converted to truth."

"But truth is relative," Timothie said, toying with his steak. The rich aroma of charred meat drifted into his nostrils, but he wasn't hungry and pushed it back. The red-lensed image of Reginald faced him across the table. He glanced around the room. All the diners had similar expressions on their faces as they ate like robots consuming a meal of potash. "Don't they know that?"

"No, of course not. They've been taught that truth is absolute. It's a cognitive dissonance," Reginald explained, cutting his potato into smaller portions and scattering bacon bits on the sour cream, then cramming the forkful into his mouth. "People have an inner need to ensure their beliefs are consistent. They'll believe what we tell them so long as it's consistent with what they already believe, with the opinions they have been fed via the Millennial Goggles, and the internet, television, movies, eBooks, everything they come into contact with, have to preach the same gospel. My sister's a pastor down in Texas. She knows that, too. They all do. It's the end of times."

"Gospel?" Timothie asked, staring at the asparagus on his platter. "Yes, I suppose it could be considered a sort of religion."

"Sure." Reginald grinned again, and his eyes sparkled as he tore off the goggles, revealing red depths in his pupils. Veins pulsed in the whites of his eyes. He cracked his knuckles. "Listen to the news. It's changed, hasn't it?"

"The leaders of our countries are afraid of nuclear war."

"The fundamentalists are right. It's the end of the world as we know it," Reginald exclaimed, and raised his fork above his head. "Hallelujah!"

"America is leading the way again. America is great again but in a sinister and apocalyptic fashion. I agree it's the end of days, Reginald. You may be the Anti-Christ."

Glasses clinked, and forks clattered on thick white plates. Timothie detected a low-pitched hum in the room. "What's that?" he asked, pushing his platter aside and sipping on a recently replenished cup of black coffee.

"I don't hear nothin'," Reginald grinned and cracked his knuckles again. He finished his meal. The box of yellow goggles jiggled on his lap.

"Is there anything I can say to stop you?" asked Timothie.

"I was hoping you'd join us," Reginald replied. "We've talked before. You're too smart not to be on the winning side, Tim. Join us. Here, try these, give them away to anyone you see who doesn't have a pair, that's what I do. People don't have to buy them. Profit isn't the point."

"You profit in men's souls," Timothie observed. "You would enslave a world of souls to serve your demigod."

Reginald's appearance wavered, and the room was a blur. Behind the man, soured and unbeaten, rose a demon with oozing black skin, black and red eyes, white pupils, and slavering deep breaths of pure poison.

Timothie gestured, and Dareboy melted through the walls carrying the Cloak of Power in his slim arms, which Timothie cast around his neck.

The cloak touched him like a protective hand caressing his skin. Spangled with silver stars, the black velvet cape enveloped the table, including Reginald, who huffed great clouds of black smoke and brimstone into the room. His encounter with Bael strengthened him. He stood up and pushed back his platter. He emptied the carafe of Riesling Spätlese Goldtröpfchen 2015 "Mosel" into his glass and gulped it all down in a splendid show of exuberance.

Dareboy stood by Timothie, shoulder to shoulder, a wall of black against Reginald's darkness. The Cloak of Power swirled. Dareboy lifted his hand and sparks arced across the table, intersecting the power of Bael's gaze now that Reginald was truly under the demon's spell. Timothie wore a patterned silver shirt and black lambskin low-rise jeans, with leather boots. Dareboy sported a black jumpsuit with white Japanese characters on the pocket and white and red Converse sneakers.

Maude appeared through the closed door, silent and intent, holding a black candle in her withered old hands. She lit it with a lighter from her bodice. Together the trio murmured in unison the spell that had been taught them on Draxxt to combat demons.

"Whatever evil comes to me here
I cast you back, I have no fear
With the speed of wind and the dark of night
May all of your harboring take flight
With the swiftness of the sea
And all the power found in me
As I will so mote it be
I CAST YOU OUT!!!!"

Dareboy blew out the black candle. Maude crossed herself. "We're all here. The force that lives within us told us you were here and needed help, my friend."

Timothie hovered above the planked floor. "Thank you." He swirled, and his leather boots caught the edge of the table.

Bael laughed. The other diners had left. The room was empty of all but close friends and servers, who seemed oblivious to the drama played out in the dining room. The maître de hovered over the table as the busboys emptied the plates onto their trays and left the room. Outside, the large clock on the old post office chimed two. The restaurant was closing.

Timothie spread his arms. Fire crackled from his fingertips. His cloak swirled and sparkled, enveloping his muscular body. Bael roared and struck out with bloody talons and gnashing incisors. Reginald's image was lost behind the thrusting demon. The smell of creosote rankled their nostrils.

Timothie soared to a corner of the room, zoomed inward to the fireplace where he picked hot coals with his bare hands and flung them at the demon, chanting an old song he had learned from Mindbender the Troll while a boy on Draxxt. Crazy Jack Dareboy joined him. The boy sprang into the air and held Timothie's arm as they both rushed at the gibbering demon, which brushed the topmost beams of the room with its head. Maude, wearing chinos and a leopard print blouse, muttered incantations she had learned as a witch on her home planet. Once again, she lit the black candle and placed it on the table.

"I CAST YOU OUT!!!" she screamed simultaneously with Dareboy and Timothie as they rushed the apparition in the corner.

"Good always wins over evil!" Timothie shouted as he punched Bael through his awful face into the back of the demon's muddy brain.

Reginald's box of remaining yellow goggles flew from the table. The servers hurried to extract them from their cases; stumbling about the room with vacant countenances. The windows rattled. Timothie's red Volvo 123 hovered and smoked outside the panes of glass. Once again, Timothie struck the demon. Bael grunted and roared but began to dissipate through the opposite walls. As it pooled into black liquid that slopped through the floorboards and walls, Reginald appeared again, disheveled and dirty.

Maude blew out the black candle. Dareboy and Timothie descended from the heights of the room. Reginald slumped over the table.

"We have to leave now," Timothie said. Behind Reginald, he threw both arms around his former friend's body and squeezed. Reginald hacked and threw up. "That's it," Timothie said. "You're full of bile, my old friend. You don't know what you've gotten yourself into."

"I do," objected Reginald, who heaved the liquid remains of his steak and potatoes into the center of the table. "It's *power*, my old pal. I won't let go of it."

"You're dead meat if you don't," observed the superhero. "I'm here to save you, Reginald, just as we're here to save the world."

"Here," Reginald gasped, holding out three pairs of yellow goggles. "Put these on. It's your only chance to avoid detection."

Attention, a tinny voice said in Timothie's brain. *Attention. All automatons report to your superiors. Now! We have detected intruders. They are our enemies. They must be assimilated.*

"What now?" asked Crazy Jack Dareboy, throwing a protective arm across Maude's shoulders. They all put on the yellow goggles, and their minds burned with the urgency of the summons. They knew that everyone in the world, everyone who wore the Millennial Goggles, heard the same directive.

Don't kill them. Bring them to me.

Invisible, Bael laughed. *I will assimilate them. The world will be mine.*

Bring them to whom? Asked the masses, crowding outside the restaurant. Wind whipped their forms into undulating waves of clothing and hair. Crows screamed from dark firs lining the avenue. Dust devils whipped through the air.

Bring them to me. My name is Justin Harper. I am your Prime Minister. Please don't let them escape. They are dangerous and will damage our new World Order. Bring them to me immediately so we may assimilate them. Then the world will be united as never before. There will be peace.

"Peace!" screamed the populace. "Peace under Harper and Ducksworth!"

"No, world peace," Reginald said and guffawed. "One money, one government, one military..."

"…and many bombs," intoned Bael from the walls. Its voice echoed as though in a sepulchre through the bones of Timothie's skull. The crowd outside crushed against the windows. The great doors opened, and the mob rushed inside.

Chapter Eighteen

As the mob streamed through the doors of the restaurant, Timothie and his friends hovered in the far upper corners of the room. The servers and chefs cowered in the back, unsure of what to do. Some called 911 on their cell phones. Sirens wailed down the avenue. The mass of yellow-goggled people crowded into Jane's Texas. Chairs smashed against the walls. Timothie and his friends dangled high above in the rafters, and Timothie suddenly laughed. The mob was unsure of itself. Groping with yellow goggles obstructing their vision, they paced like automatons into the corners, blindly searching for the perpetrators of disruption of world unity.

"Hey, Tim," called Dareboy, his black jumpsuit with crimson logos on the arms superbly outlining his supple frame. "Here come de judge!" He yelled with glee and threw a fistful of electrical bolts from his outstretched fingers to the leaders of the mob. They fell back in disarray, their jackets scorched.

A stout woman with blonde hair screamed, "I'm Maude's friend!" and disintegrated into black cinders. Maude unsizzled her to life again.

"I think they would easily be bowled over with a breath from Uriel." Timothie's black cloak swirled. A chef appeared from the kitchen and threw a large pot of boiling pasta on the frontrunners, who fell back, rigatoni dripping from their faces.

"Take that, infidels!" screamed a waiter and impaled a thin man with a carving knife. Another waiter flailed his arms in the direction of Timothie's friends, who swooped from the ceiling onto the mass of enraged yellow-goggled people. "Get out of our establishment! This is a classy place! You pigs!" he cried.

The mob began to fight among itself as Timothie, Dareboy, and Reginald hid behind the sudden enveloping wings of Uriel. The door banged shut, and the mob screamed against the locks, trying to shatter the windows as the huge white Angel pinions suffocated the whole mass of Ducksworth worshippers. They threw down their yellow goggles and shouted, "Death to Bael!"

"What did we say?" asked the stout man in the dark glasses. "Death to whom?"

"Death to Bael!" answered his companion, elbowing him. "We've seen the might of the Angel. It's is God's answer to the anti-Christ!"

"Who's that?" asked someone else, elbowing and shoving his way to the open doors.

"Glad there's no children here," commented Crazy Jack Dareboy before he threw another bolt of lightning from his outstretched fingers. Timothie nodded, smirked, and swirled above the mob dispensing a deluge of battery acid onto their heads, which didn't seem to injure them but stung like fire in their eyes.

"You win!" cried the mob. The chefs chased them outside, then locked the doors with heavy bolts. The intact windows were smeared with fingerprints of humans who desperately tried to escape. The sirens Timothie had heard ground to a halt outside the restaurant. Two sturdy boys in uniform pounded on the doors. Jane's Texas was a shambles.

"What's going on here?" asked the sergeant, pushing into the room as a server unlocked the door.

"Just a mob," replied the sous chef. "It's gone now."

"Just a mob? What were they doing in a steakhouse? Did you have a special and then lock the doors?"

"No, cop, they were after some peaceful customers. We made short shrift of them."

Battery acid dripped from the rafters. The cops wiped their faces, and one replaced his hat. "Are we needed here? We got a call from the kitchen."

"I think, if anything, you need to arrest those leaders of the mob who are escaping down the street. You'll know them. They're wearing yellow goggles."

The policeman whipped out a pair of his own yellow goggles. "Like these? Long live Dennis Ducksworth."

"You're too much, sir," shouted Dareboy and swooped from the ceiling. He landed directly in front of the sergeant. "Put on those yellow goggles and immerse yourself in Never Never Land, if you choose. We choose to fight for liberty and God."

"Sounds good," said the other cop, pulling the goggles off his companion. "I love the game, though doubt the outcome."

"Do you have maybe more education than this other officer?" Timothie asked. He smirked and waved his brawny hand in front of the sergeant's face.

"Yes, I came into the force with a B.Sc. in chemistry," said the other.

"Makes you think," acknowledged Timothie. "Though education is overrated. I'm sure you learn as much on the beat as you did in college."

"Not much," replied the first, and the second reached for his goggles. "You're not under arrest, fellows, but you must vacate the premises. We'll send someone out to interview the owners. Meanwhile, let's pick up this mess, shall we, servers?"

The mighty white pinions of the Angel reappeared, invisible to the officers, and swept up in one motion the overturned tables, the dismantled chairs, and the broken dishes. The servers quickly set everything to rights with the help of the Divine breath in the room. The cops left, mumbling, and the second one straightened the goggles on his face while the first officer continued to expound against the use of them, quoting his college education and the ability it had given him to think things through. The first cop, the sergeant, slid into the driver's seat of the black and white police car. They accelerated down the street, siren blaring. The other two cars followed, weaving in and out of traffic on their way to Tim Horton's.

"That's done," exclaimed Reginald. "I'm so sorry, Timothie, I didn't mean to have the mob turn on you like that. I just wanted you to join us peacefully, not by force."

"Hey, Reginald," shouted Dareboy, leaning on the newly pressed white tablecloth. "Do you remember what day it is?"

"All I know is it's Sunday," replied Reginald, pulling on his thin blond mustache. "And it's the twenty-first day of May, I think, Crazy Jack. Why? OH!!!" He exclaimed, jumped up, and clapped his hands. "Timothie's birthday!"

Timothie ducked his head. "I had made arrangements for a party here," he admitted. "It was great. But this blew it all out of the water."

"A party!" exclaimed Dareboy. "Let's have a better one now!"

He snapped his fingers, and Reg's father appeared, slouched in a corner chair smiling, just like Timothie. Another "POP" and Gianni Simoni transported all the way from Rome where he was spending holidays. He leaned on a pillar and smiled. The quiet man and his partner, Bill popped into view. Other friends: the woman in the plaid shirt, the stunning woman in the red dress, the tall cowboy, and more, all crowded into Jane's Texas Steakhouse, again to celebrate Timothie's fiftieth birthday. The servers brought out wine, beer, diet Pepsi, and coffee. A huge cake dripped with whipped cream and roses. *Happy 50th Birthday, Timothie.*

Left behind on the floor were a hundred pair of yellow goggles. Bael slunk from under the floorboards and devoured them.

"Give up yet, demon?" yelled Crazy Jack Dareboy.

Maude screamed with delight and struck her wrinkled hands onto the writhing form in the room. Purple lightning singed the black, white, and red liquid that was Bael. Uriel smiled and placed her pale hands into the ooze. Bael screamed and wound itself into a ball, then disappeared in a hiss of smoke.

Timothie munched. "This cake is delicious."

"Happy birthday, old friend. It only gets better after this," assured Maude. She stroked her ash blonde pixie cut and applied Iris Apfel pink lipstick to her smiling lips.

"You should know." Reginald shrugged. "I have work to do after this. I think my game needs tweaking."

"You're kidding," Dareboy said. "You're still intent on taking over the world?"

Reginald smiled. His eyes glowed. He cracked his knuckles. "Of course," he said. "The game has only begun."

"You've lost a battle," observed Bill, the thin man's partner. "I'm feeling better now, after the other night. I threw away my Millennial goggles, Reg."

"Better than that, you stopped smoking," said his partner. Bill nodded and smiled, then coughed again.

"Didn't work for too long," he said, reached in his pocket, and pulled out a pack of menthol cigarettes.

"But I haven't lost the war," Reginald declared, and slunk out the door. On his way out, he picked up a pair of the undamaged goggles and threw them onto his face. His eyes glowed red through the lenses.

"Do you think we've seen the last of him?" asked Dareboy. He gulped on a Heineken beer and shoved a piece of cheese into his mouth.

"No way," said Timothie. "This cake is delicious. Who baked it?"

"I did," said Maude and smiled. "Was up all night with it."

The woman in plaid reached into a trash can and pulled out a plastic cake container with a label. "What's this?"

"It says Italian Bakery," observed Timothie. "But we all know that my friend Maude was up all night baking this. I've never tasted better German Chocolate Cake."

"I think it's Black Forest," said Maude.

"You should know," said Timothie. "Good whipped cream and cherries."

"You are a duckie," cooed Maude and wiped the side of his face with her freckled hand. "I love you."

They all sang "For He's a Jolly Good Fellow" and Reginald's father took his leave.

Reginald glowered through the window. He wore the yellow goggles. Down the street, a car backfired.

"Was that a gunshot?" the snazzy lady in the red dress asked.

"Of course," laughed Dareboy and helped himself to another piece of the delicious dripping cake. "You must get used to it. We're in danger here."

"Not danger," said Timothie, delighted. "Adventure."

Chapter Nineteen

Some issues are unspoken, but they should not remain that way. One was Uriel's interference in the affairs of the 21st century, wherein Timothie and his friends fought and sometimes bled for a righteous cause.

A quieter day ensued after the impromptu second birthday party at Jane's Texas Steakhouse. Timothie and his two good friends from a faraway planet and time, Maude and Dareboy, lounged on his leather couch and recliner chair in the apartment on Ada Boulevard. His new Roku television flickered with Sunday images. Timothie believed he ought to follow the current news, in view of recent events.

A crystal palace brimmed with worshippers from California. The television evangelist's face was blank with ignorance about the new Canadian Prime Minister, Justin Dale Harper, who had so recently been all over Canadian news threatening world domination. The preacher's message was distorted by yellow goggles and a mouth full of platitudes.

Timothie picked at his cloak. Dareboy smirked and raised his glass of diet Pepsi. Suddenly the evangelist's form wavered and disappeared. A cloud of purple smoke issued from the screen, replaced a moment later by flakes of feather and snow. Uriel hovered before them.

"Only good can come of this visit," exclaimed Timothie and held out his cloak with silver stars. "What do you want from me, oh you great and powerful Christ's messenger?"

"Thank you, dude." Dareboy set down his glass, swirling wet rings on the table's surface. "We couldn't have done it without you. But it seems our efforts are balked by evil at every turn, though as my friend Tim would say, good will overcome evil."

Uriel bowed her great head. "It seems you need my help."

"You're an Angel, right?" Dareboy grasped a corner of the Cloak of Power. Silver stars cascaded into the room. "I know how the technological landscape is affecting our foreign compatriot countries. Everyone's affected by this neuromarketing. Social media spreads it like a fire out of control, or a tsunami washing the borders of ourselves and our allies away into an ocean of automatons. Our fellow countrymen are robots, and they're damaging the fabric of civilization itself."

"Our American friends were the first to be affected," Timothie commented. "Next Canada and the U.K. fell. It spread all over Europe, Asia, and Africa, as well as Australia and New Zealand. We are wretched mortals, and this is a demigod of evil that's been spawned by my former friend Reginald Smith. He still shows up now and then, and I keep my enemies close. But we narrowly escaped danger yesterday, and I'm afraid for Earth. It could even spread beyond Earth, to our home planet."

"Are you afraid for yourself or for your world?" whispered the great form of Uriel, bowing low in the high-ceilinged room.

"I'm afraid for Timothie and Dareboy," Maude burst out. "They're my friends and don't understand the magic that can keep them whole. But my magic won't spread over the entire Earth. My magic can't protect all citizens of this country and the next, or the rest of the world. The universe may be doomed without your help, Uriel."

"Timothie has Christ's help to defeat the storms of evil that Bael has released," confirmed the Angel. She gestured with a mighty hand, and a golden cross blazed from her palm to the middle of Timothie's Cloak of Power. The trio of mortals huddled around the blazing symbol.

Uriel's wings stirred. "This will protect you as I do. Go forth tonight and decide on your course of action, but don't overthink, good friends. We work as one team. Wisdom lies in simplicity. Maude has the magic. Jack Dareboy has charisma and power. Timothie has the goodness of Heaven and both magic and power. Use your gifts to best advantage.

This golden cross will burn in Heaven's midst and call me when you need me. Good night, my good friends. I go back to protect the salon." She disappeared, leaving a few wisps of snowy feathers on the carpet.

Timothie stood tall and muscular in the middle of his living room. The Roku smart TV flickered and screamed out the evangelist's distorted rants. Dareboy bounced up from his reclining position on the coffee-colored sofa and snapped off the set with the remote control. Maude threw her crystals from a small velvet bag. They sparkled in the evening air. Bands of crimson and gold settled over the southwest river valley, the golf course below still home to tiny moving figures.

"We have to talk," Timothie said. "I think these goggles should be federally regulated and stored in gun safes when not in use."

"In use for what?" Crazy Jack Dareboy threw a dark arm around Maude's sloping shoulders. "They should be banned completely. Somehow Reginald and his demon are inciting the population of the whole Earth to respond to the American leaders, who are obviously under the control of Hell itself."

Timothie swirled. He peered at himself in the marbled mirror that leaned against one wall. "Until now, the technology of neuromarketing was not available to the general populace nor the leaders. I suspect the military had the capacity, but it wasn't misused on a vast scale as it is now. We have to make a plan. There's only the three of us."

"There are more," Maude objected. "Many more on our side, Timothie. If we recruit them to our cause, we'll be stronger in numbers."

"We don't necessarily need the numbers. I'm convinced the universe is taking care of us. We just have to plug into the magic that's out there, the good that's coming down the tube from Heaven."

Dareboy hovered a few feet above the carpet. Maude threw a handful of crystals onto the shining tabletop. Colors from the setting sun sparkled across the room. Shining prisms from dew streaked windows cast rainbows onto the white walls.

Timothie whispered, "I think we're out of touch with the news and with social media. I'll appoint myself to investigate the online world of information, which is vast, as you know, and we don't know what news is being fed into those yellow goggles. Now that I have some news channels to watch and my Android data to keep up with, I'll do that more consistently. But the yellow goggles broadcast information we don't know."

"Oh, but we do," declared Crazy Jack, zipping upwards by three or four feet and extending his arms like wings. "I wear them a lot."

"No wonder you're so mad," muttered Maude. As though in another world, she murmured incantations to herself while sorting the crystals.

"Why are you exempted from their magic, Dareboy?" asked Timothie. "To me, that's suspicious."

"Oh, you don't trust your old friend?" Dareboy smirked and continued to hover. He snapped the remote control, and the television roared to life. Timothie flinched.

"We'll go to the United Nations with our concerns," he said. "They should know what's trying to destroy the nations of the world."

"Yes, that's the ticket." Dareboy flicked the channel changer. "Why, here they are now. It's President Dennis Ducksworth's European tour."

"See what we have to contend with," continued Timothie. "See what we can do."

Crazy Jack cackled and clicked together his Dubarry Kerry leather ankle boots. "Yes. See what you can do."

The golden cross flared in the middle of the Cloak of Power. Shining rays of setting sunlight gilded the Wassily Kandinsky print over the sofa. Brilliant cushions flashed with coordinating colors as Timothie settled into the recliner. He pushed back the soft leather arms.

"Give me the remote," he ordered and peered at his Android phone. "I'm going to text the heart of Geneva, Switzerland." He extended a tanned hand and caught the remote that Crazy Jack tossed to him. "There's an emergency channel open for civilians. I'm going to use it."

"First you should see what's going on there." Dareboy laughed. The sun descended further in the southwest, throwing the apartment into shadows. Half a mile down, in the river valley, the golfers went home. "There's eight hours difference between the United Nations in Geneva and here in Edmonton. Good thing the news says they're sitting early on what is tomorrow in Switzerland. They'll be at it now."

"Look," Maude urged. A small electrical storm raged amongst her crystals and touched the Android. "Look at the screen, Timothie."

He touched his mobile's small screen. Blue light sizzled between his Android and the crystals. Maude continued to chant. Dareboy hovered and smirked. The Roku's 52-inch screen flashed a picture of the United Nations Office in Geneva and illuminated the heads of state sitting there. Timothie gasped.

Dennis Ducksworth of the U.S.A. held them in the palm of his hand with his oratory, and without exception, the leaders of the nations all wore yellow goggles.

Chapter Twenty

Monday, the first week in May, was another day off. Timothie laced up his white leather Converse runners and popped a white Converse baseball hat onto his salt and pepper hair. Smiling, he took a selfie of himself in skinny, stretchy khakis and flowered shirt with the sleeves taken off to accommodate his biceps. He posted it to Facebook, where friends with yellow goggles admired his muscles.

Yellow goggles. He swiped a hand through his hair, lifting the cap as he did so. Skye had given him a pair of the goggles, and so had Reginald. Their powers needed attention, and he placed the goggles on his face as he prepared to chase away cobwebs down Ada Boulevard for his early morning run. Sure enough. The software had been updated since he last tried the goggles.

A kaleidoscope of color greeted him, and a soft voice murmured in his ear, over and over, a mantra of political correctness and a chant joined by millions of other voices over the world, in many dialects, but all with the same message:

"We are one. Follow the flow. Follow the flow. We are one. Peace to the world through bombs. Bombs. Bombs. Follow the flow. Follow the flow. Ducksworth shall lead. Ducksworth shall lead. I will follow. I will follow. Peace to the world. Follow Ducksworth. We are one. We are one. Follow. Follow the flow."

All the while, his mind pieced together the varied images that flashed from the bottom of his vision to the top, to the left and right, and back again so that he could see beyond the images to the sidewalk, through the red lenses, in a red haze. The chanting took hold of his mind until finally…

In a fit of rebelliousness, Timothie snatched the glasses from his face. He stowed them in a pocket, afraid someone vulnerable may pick them up if he threw them away. Not that anyone invulnerable was left in the world, he thought. *All my neighbors and foreign countries are tuned into nuclear warfare and even worship the bomb that Ducksworth promises, including peace on his terms as a united world under his rule, according to the demigod Bael.*

The goggles whispered their neuroscience to all, including the President of the United States and the convergence of all leaders at the United Nations. Timothie wiped the perspiration from his forehead, which continued to stream as he ran. And ran.

He pelted down Ada Boulevard, turned the corner, and soon found himself running up 50 Street to 118 Avenue and then to his empty salon. There he turned the key in the lock and slammed the door shut after him. He flicked on the lights and threw the goggles into the back room where Skye and Paula could find them in the morning. Rummaging through the fridge in the kitchen, Timothie extracted a can of diet Pepsi and some sausage and cheese, which he stuffed into his mouth as though not to starve the intelligence still left in his brain.

The herd instinct was strong. Only those who were wired differently from the general population could survive. The bipolar, schizophrenic, the autistic, the extremely creative, the very young and elderly without computers or the desire to join social media or new technology, only they would escape. Diet Pepsi dribbled down Timothie's chin onto his flowered shirt and over the dark hairs on his arm. He drew his mobile Android from his back pocket and tapped out Dareboy's number.

"What's up, dude?" His friend's handsome face appeared almost instantly. "It's your day off, isn't it? Want another repeat of Sunday? Watch a bit of TV, get high on angels and the political situation, maybe? Scary stuff, isn't it?"

"Yeah," Timothie answered, thumbing through the data on his phone. "I guess. Want to get together this afternoon, Crazy Jack?"

"Don't call me that," Dareboy replied and frowned. "I told you that before. It's probably the only reason I escaped what I see and feel with the Millennial Goggles."

"That's what they call them now?"

"I don't know. It's what I call them. Reginald calls them the Millennial Goggles, but first he named them Prototype B. Something to do with Hell and Heaven, and we know what side he's on."

"We sure do," Timothie said. "It's all coming to a head now. It seems like only a few brave souls are not affected."

"Like your friend Maude. She's too old to be interested in high-tech stuff."

"I don't think so. I think she's just different. Not wired that way, like I'm not, and I think she has friends her age who wouldn't be interested in social media or the whispers of a demigod through new science."

"I think so. She's a stand-up woman. Maybe, like you say, she has friends like her? Maybe we could get them all together, you know, the Grey Warriors or the Silver Squad, and get them to combat the craziness in the world now. All over the world, we could recruit the baby boomers and war babies. What do you say?"

"How do we do that?" Timothie mused as he thumbed his Android. The Pepsi turned warm in his hand. "You're right, though, there's more of them than there are of us in the general population. And they're a crazy bunch. Went through three centuries, two millennia, the fifties, the sixties, the crazy seventies, all those wars, they all went through major world-wide financial depressions. They're a tough bunch of broads."

"Don't forget the men."

"Oh, yes, the men," Timothie said. "War heroes, many of them, farm workers, CEOs and managers, technicians and tradesmen from a by-gone past. Harder workers and smarter than the millennials and don't forget Generation X."

"No, they've bought into the new order."

Timothie frowned. "Don't be so sure. But we have the Baby Boomers."

"Maude? Yes, she has friends. She lives in a seniors' lodge, attends church regularly, and she also knows a lot of people from her whist club that meets every Wednesday. Let's mobilize the grey troops. Crazy," Dareboy continued and clicked off. His face disappeared from Timothie's small screen.

Lost in thought for a few minutes, Timothie sank into the silver chair in front of his hanging mirror. The sun streamed through the open blinds and bathed the ivy which climbed the walls of the salon in golden green hues. His Android lay still in his hands. Finally, he lifted his head, threw his white Converse hat across the room, and dialed Maude's number at home.

She answered on the fourth ring.

"Let's all get together again," she said, after hearing him out. "We need a plan."

"Can you help?"

Her raucous laughter echoed through the room from the mobile's speakers. "Of course, dear, I can help. But we need a battle plan."

"A battle plan. Yes."

"Yeah, dear one. This is war."

Chapter Twenty-One

"Meet my friends," Maude declared the next day, Timothie's second day off. A motley group of grey and silver-haired elders crowded into Timothie's rooms on the top floor of the mansion on Ada Boulevard. "My friend Susan's brother," Maude continued. "She was the gal in the bright red dress at the party, with the Cowboy." A blondish man of average height and stocky athletic build stepped forward. His bright blue eyes were wide in a happy face. He thrust a hand like a ham into Timothie's outstretched hand.

"Santiago Florian. Nice to meet you."

"I didn't know your friend was Spanish, Maude," Dareboy said. "Her brother isn't the typical Spaniard, either."

"They're third generation Canadian, dude," Maude replied and smiled at Santiago. "But you'd never know it around their family table. The Florians are a noble old Spanish family with a suitable coat of arms to prove it. Her bro is very proud of their heritage. More so since he's not the typical olive skinned Spaniard, I think!"

Dareboy swung down from his perch in the top corner of the room above the arc lamp. He loved to hover and frighten the guests. "Ah. There was a Viking in the woodpile."

"Well, we're not sure who our father is," acknowledged Santiago.

The woman in the red dress sidled up to Maude and ran brown fingers through her ashen hair. "But I'm pretty sure we're Florians."

"Got anything to drink here?" her brother asked. His wife, Patricia Florian, a slim woman with rimless glasses and blunt cut hair, nudged him with her foot. Timothie disappeared into the kitchen to mix up a pitcher of Sangria.

Maude smiled again. "Patricia plays banjo alongside Santiago, dances flamenco, bikes, hikes, walks, kayaks; they're a couple made in heaven."

Timothie was polite. "Where do you work, Patricia?"

"She has a degree in linguistics," Santiago volunteered, slurping on a thick glass of red Sangria and putting a muscular arm around his wife.

"Romance languages," she corrected him. "I worked at the U.N. as a translator in New York before I retired. Maude thinks my training could be useful to help decode the Millennial Goggles."

"Or understand what's going on at the U.N. now," Maude said as Santiago passed her a small glass of sherry.

"Interesting," Timothie said. "Do you all know why we're here?"

"Sure," the group chorused in unison. "We're the Grey Squad."

"The Silver Warriors," corrected a stooped woman with a walker. Her white hair was in contrast to her youthful face. "I've had two knee replacements, but I can still outrun that sloppy demon from Hell you've told me about, Timothie."

Timothie threw a leg over the side of the coffee-colored leather sofa and opened a can of diet Pepsi with a *ping*. "Or Reginald Smith. Who else is in?"

"Count me in, honey," volunteered a woman with short white curly hair, large droopy breasts and a perky butt, gorgeous hooded brown eyes, and plentiful exuberant hugs. She bounced about on small dainty feet. "I might have a bad back but my heart is strong."

Dareboy was keeping count on a small tablet he propped up on his knee. "Name?"

"Julie Ann Carter," she declared. "At your service, honey. And this here handsome brown-eyed farmer is Ross Murray, with his wife, Jenny. She was an R.N. back in the day, and a good one, too. Ever hear of the Member of Parliament for South Peace whose life she saved? Or he swears that she did."

"Oh, I'm just a stupid little woman," Jenny said but beamed. She put a proprietary hand on her taller husband's shoulder. "I always considered my patients my children. Just loved them."

"They were never blessed with kids," explained Maude and waved her arm to take in the rest of the room. "Here we all are, but there's more, too. I belong to an active big Baptist church on the south side and attend every Sunday. Also, there's my Wednesday morning whist group that meets in the Manor, not to mention the folks in the Manor itself. Quite a large group, and none of us connected to social media except maybe Patricia there, who'll need it to manage those idjits at the U.N."

"With their yellow goggles," confirmed a short, rotund man of American heritage. "Huh, they all systematically began to take away our freedoms after the Gulf War. Don't trust any of them. And the leaders of the countries in the free world aren't any better. I didn't vote for them."

"You didn't vote at all," Maude reminded and winked. "I know that for a fact. You have dual nationality, Ben O'Hara, and you don't pay U.S. taxes, nor do you vote. For shame."

"I don't make enough to pay taxes," grumbled the old curmudgeon. "And there's nobody worth voting for on the slate since Jimmy Carter."

"Still, you're a strong force on our Silver Warriors team, Ben," declared Dareboy, looking up from his racing fingers on the tablet. "You have knowledge of the American system and possibly how Dennis Ducksworth got voted in. We could use you."

"Thanks," Ben murmured and sat down. In one hand he nursed a Scotch, humorous blue eyes sparkling behind thick lenses. "You know, Maude, if he put together all the electronics "on" lights in this room, we could make a Christmas tree."

"Yes, Timothie, turn on the lamps," urged Dareboy and settled on a Danish style footstool, flicking on a table light as he did so. "Don't you think we ought to invite Reginald along, too? After all, he knows more about the Millennial Goggles than anyone, he created the software program and presumably the updates. What's his agenda? We have to know before we launch a counterattack."

The entrepreneur crossed her long limbs and leaned against her brother's shoulder on the leather sofa. "My late husband used to say keep your enemies close so you can keep an eye on them."

"I say that, too," Timothie mused, flicking his thumbs over his Android screen. "Here, this is interesting. I just tried to call Reginald at home and got this instead." He held up the small monitor for all the room to see. Flames flickered at the edges of the screen and the speakers screeched. An image of Reginald melted into the flames.

"Where is he?" asked Dareboy, continuing to take a census of the Silver Warriors in the room. "Looks like Hell."

"It's that demon he conjures up, I'm sure," Timothie said. "He's taken over the apartment. There's a pentagram on the floor tiles, and Reg has incantations and holy water that keep him pretty well contained, but he's a powerful force and one not to be trifled with."

"What's its agenda?" Santiago asked, swirling the Sangria in his glass. His wife gently took the glass from him.

"That's enough, dear," she murmured. He frowned and hitched up his chino trousers, his smooth-shaven face serious.

"No, I mean it, dude, what does this thing want from us? Why are all the Millennials and Generation X wearing these stupid yellow goggles, and what do they hope to get from it? We can pull our weight as elders – the growing age gap, gender ratios, and other key takeaways are clear. Statistics say that seniors account for almost seventeen percent of Canada's population. We outnumber children. We can force our agenda by sheer force of numbers if we all get together. But it has to be worldwide. This little gathering here in your condo doesn't cut it, Timothie. We have to get on our phones and Apples and alert the rest of the world."

"How are we going to do that?" asked Ben, setting down his half-sipped glass of Scotch. "Aren't we enough here, with the expertise we have and the energy that's in this room?"

"Not to mention our magic." Dareboy smirked from his corner of the room and winked at Maude. She rattled her crystals in the little velvet bag and threw a wicked glance around the room. Blue lightning sizzled in the close air, electric with potential and challenge. Dareboy raised a hand and streaks of power crackled through his fingers.

"So, what about our friend Reginald?" asked Timothie from his place by the window. "It appears he's not answering his cell, and he's conjured up the demon again. What does he plan to do this time? We all know Bael's ultimate purpose is to get as many human souls as he can to fight the final battle with Heaven and usurp God's throne for himself. It's a plot worthy of Hell itself that is doomed to failure. Because good will always overcome evil. But the world may become its battlefield before that happens. The universe could turn on the world and destroy us all, as conspirators for Hell's demons."

"That's true," acknowledged a new firm voice, and they all turned to look at the medium-sized man with short blond hair and mustache who appeared before them.

"Reginald!" exclaimed Patricia. "I'd know you anywhere from Tim's description."

"I'm a very nondescript sort of fellow," Reginald said. "But the power I hold is more than you can imagine. Take this, losers!" He held in his hand a small pool of black liquid that oozed out through his fingers. He threw the foul concoction into the air, and it hung, shining with slime and rot for ten seconds before it slithered like a mythological serpent onto the floor and wrapped itself around the legs of all there, a boiling black, white, and red tar baby of putridness.

"So, it's come to this!" called Maude and began to chant. She threw her velvet bag of crystals into the center of the boiling mess. Lightning arced from her fingertips and she *danced* into the middle of the demon's heaving form.

Bael slurped and slobbered. A maniac cackled and screamed where Reginald had stood a moment before. A box of yellow goggles under its arm upended and dissolved in the steaming vapor that was Bael.

"All hail Bael!" screamed the figure that had been Reginald.

"Look what you've done," moaned the friend with the walker.

"Be quiet, Heather Ellen Armstrong. My husband's an old soldier. He fought in the war and came back to his country, and he's not going to let any demon from Hell tell us what to do in a free country," cried Jenny Murray, her dark hair that hadn't yet turned grey wild about her wrinkled face. "Ross will protect us!"

Ross Murray, a tall man with a widow's peak and silver hair, appeared startled but soon pulled himself together and put an arm around his wife.

"Jenny, I think we're in over our heads. We should ask that fellow over there if he knows how to clean up this mess and that screaming thing over there that used to be a man. Do they still talk about the war in school? We need some younger blood here."

"Ross, you can help us." His wife clamped her lips together and folded her arms in front of her. "If you won't do something, I will." She took a step forward, and her slippers fell into the heaving slime that was Bael. She took another step and leaned down to pick up a pair of yellow goggles that hadn't yet dissolved. She began to pray out loud. "*Yay, though I walk through the valley of the shadow of death, I shall fear no evil...*"

Then she began to sing "The Old Rugged Cross." Maude crossed herself. The entire room took up the old hymn. As they stood, they swayed and held hands until they formed a circle around Bael and Reginald with the old nurse in the middle of the pile. Their voices reached the rafters. A crescendo of music filled the room, "*On a hill far away, stood an old rugged cross...*"

Ross Murray grinned. "*...an old Model A...*" he sang in a very atonal tenor. The room took up the hymn again then went on to others, all the ancient hymns of their childhood. Some crossed themselves, and others prayed according to their inclinations and faith. The room filled with incense as Dareboy lit a pile of sticks in a burner. Acrid smoke curled up to the rafters, and Dareboy and Timothie in his Cloak of Power hovered again above the crowd. Someone opened a window.

"We're the mighty Silver Warriors," they sang, "Nothing can defeat us. Statistics reveal we are what we feel – seventeen percent of the world!"

That was enough. The monster that had been Reginald wavered and slouched back into human form, a pair of yellow goggles crooked on his face. Flashing reds, oranges, purples, and blues reflected in the irises of his eyes like flames shooting from his brain. He screamed and hummed along... *soft as the voice of an angel... whispering Hope...* then Santiago and Patricia took up their instruments, mandolin and banjo, and began to play.

The huge lake of black, red, and white eyes heaved on the floor, disengaged itself from their ankles, and began to whimper into a small puddle again. Reginald held out his hands, and the puddle leaped into his grasp. It dripped between his fingers. With quick movements, the hero of the day, Jenny Murray, shook off the remnants of slime from her slippers and stepped into the arms of her husband. Ross hugged his wife and patted her back. "My protector," she murmured. "Nobody will ever love me as much as you do."

"She's a good woman," Ben O'Hara stated. His voice had rocked the room. Heather Ellen Armstrong seemed to stand taller, her voice like an opera aria soared over the dying strains of "Amazing Grace."

"They both sing in the Darling Clementines choir for seniors," explained Maude. She gathered up her crystals. They were still wet but shining with fire. Dareboy's face flamed with exuberance.

"I'm so happy," he said. "We've proven we could do it. You were transformed, Reginald. I think you became a demon yourself. Doesn't that bother you?"

Reginald dropped the handful of slime into a cup from his backpack. "Yes," he said. "It does. But I have a world to conquer, Crazy Jack, and what do you have as a goal?"

"We're keeping you close," laughed Timothie, and the gold cross gleamed on his black cloak. The silver stars cascaded from his shoulders. He swirled like a lithe ancient Greek god and spread his arms wide. "We have a world to conquer, too, Reginald, but it's different from the evil universe you have conjured up. We have a world of peace and goodness to lift up to the skies, and to welcome in a new age for eternity. That's a worthy goal. What is your goal but to become a toady to a foreign power that wants nothing better than to devour you and others like you in its quest for immortality?"

"It will give us immortality, too, and glory," declared Reginald, slinking out the door into the hallway carpeted with brocade rugs. "I didn't tell you. I was made CEO and President of the world-wide organization of TopStrategy Marketing. The sky's the limit for us. They do what I say. I've made them billions. Billions. And they're all wearing the yellow goggles."

"Congratulations, genius," said Julie Ann Carter as she hugged Heather Ellen. "Enjoy the thrill while you can. Because the higher you go, the harder you'll fall."

"It's time to get together with the rest of the seventeen percent," Ben O'Hara declared.

"You're a psychologist, Ben," said Maude. "Or you were before you retired. What should we do first?"

"We've already discussed the stats part," Ben replied. "We have to know our strengths and weaknesses. Then elect a leader. Or do that first. Then designate the leaders of each group so we can work on our strengths and fill in people to take care of the gaps in our strengths. Every group has a weakness. It's our job to see that everyone is used to their full potential. Nobody is left behind. We'll all pull together. Positive outcomes come from positive actions."

"We need to know what we're up against. Dareboy and Timothie, you know the risks and dangers more than anyone. Who will lead us to victory?" asked Maude.

"You will," declared Timothie and snapped shut his Android on a swirl of fire within.

"I can't," said Maude. "I don't have all the facts. Nor the leadership abilities. Not like you do, Timothie."

"I'm no leader," objected Timothie. "Maybe Dareboy, if not Maude? Someone with magic."

"Yes, someone with an Angel on our side and a Cloak of Power that gleams with a golden cross." Santiago and his wife, Patricia, pushed forward and began to strum, legs akimbo, and sang with rousing voices an old civil war song.

Mine eyes have seen the glory of the coming of the Lord… he is trampling out the vintage where the grapes of wrath are stored…

…his terrible swift sword…

…his truth goes marching on…

Santiago drummed on his guitar, the mandolin left behind in a corner of a velveteen chair. His wife braced her legs and sang in a clear, strong voice.

The lights flickered, and huge white pinions brushed behind the open windows, which were dark as Timothie's cloak and sprinkled with golden stars. A full moon swung between purple clouds in a pale, sweaty glory of craters. They could clearly see its face.

Uriel's whisper filled the entire room and boomed backward into the night. "I am with you early and late, morning and night. Have no fear."

Timothie wept. "Can you spread the word to the entire world, to the elders of every society, so that we may act in one accord like the Disciples did?"

Yes, Uriel murmured, dipped her mighty head in acquiescence, then swooped southwards with Dareboy on her back.

Chapter Twenty-Two

With Dareboy flown away on Uriel's back, there was nothing for Timothie to do but take charge. So, he swirled in his cloak with the burning cross and silver stars sprinkled about its expanse. The Silver Warriors watched wide-eyed as he took a stand in front of the now empty front window, wearing black Levi 501s and white shirt open at the top, with the sleeves cut off. He wore black sandals and a Blackstone cap.

"Let's bow to the man," called Ben. "He'll tell us what to do and where to go on our quest to rid the world of evil."

"Yes," they echoed, "He is the man of the hour."

Ross Murray eased his long back into a velveteen armchair. He tapped with his cane on the parquet floor beside him. "My friend," he murmured, and his wife pursed her lips and sat up straighter than she had before, though leaning toward him.

"He means his cane," she explained, but no one was listening. All eyes were on Timothie.

What to do? Timothie knew he was now the leader, but he had no idea how to proceed. Reginald had slunk away long before Uriel's departure, with Bael leaving a wet spot on the floor. White curtains flapped in the breeze from the open window. The sixties-style floor lamp glowed with a yellow sheen onto the assortment of seniors huddled on the floor, the sofa, the velveteen chairs, and some even perched on tables. The room was full. Timothie knew that he must speak to make them bold.

"Darlings," he began, and they nodded expectantly. "We're here to celebrate our uniqueness. We don't rely on the world wide web, we don't carry cell phones unless for emergencies, we use a pen to write on a paper tablet and not an electronic cursor. We are old school, and that is our strength."

"What's this 'we'?" asked Santiago. "You seem young enough, and I notice a lot of electronics on your shelf, and an Android you keep glancing at as though to reassure yourself that you're still connected to la la land."

Maude smiled. "Not only that, but some of us are more with it than you might think, my friend. I know I use a mobile phone and I have a PC at home that is connected to Wi-Fi. We are not all old hat. But I know what you're saying. We're not glued to the screens like our children and grandchildren are. We can talk to each other across the table. We distrust new technology, as a rule, though some of us do embrace it. What do you intend to do with such an assortment of backward citizens?"

"You're right," Timothie acknowledged. "Dareboy, Reginald, and I are young enough to get caught up in the neuromarketing that's going on with that game that's gone viral across the world. But we haven't, and neither has our friend, Gianni, though he owns more than one pair of goggles. Some of us are just naturally immune."

"Those are the sorts we have to get on our side," Santiago declared, arm around Patricia. "As well as the army of Silver Warriors, as you put it, though I don't like to group us all into one camp like that. Not all of us are old and decrepit." And he threw a glance sideways at a couple of seniors who were bent and rather vacant. "Even those would surprise you," he continued.

"We can use us all," Timothie said. "It's just a matter of time before we discover our individual strengths and weaknesses. Now I want you all to break into groups of three or four and elect a leader, who will take notes. We'll pass out pencils and paper, or you can use a tablet if you have one."

Ben grunted and began to distribute pads of paper and pencils, which he first sharpened with a small penknife. Jenny and Maude chose a slim woman who wore an Oilers jersey and earrings to be in their group. They were joined by a red-haired, sturdy woman with a German accent and round face. The four of them, being rather healthy and fitter than some, huddled on a rug in front of the leather sofa.

"Maude, you take notes," Jenny said, and Maude gripped her cell phone.

"I have data on this," she said.

"Amusing," the German woman commented and laughed. "I don't even know what you mean."

Maude ran her left hand through ash-colored hair that was beginning to show darker roots. "We don't have to use paper."

"Oh."

The others in the room divided themselves into groups of three and four and began to converse in low tones. They argued and debated from dark corner chairs and tables strewn with yellow light, to the more comfortable sofa where Ben, Ross, and Timothie huddled. Finally, in louder voices, they seemed to be making progress with the logistics of forming a cohesive plan that would defeat the world leaders who whispered their neuroscience into the bowels of the viral game that the greater percentage of the population played.

The gleaming wooden clock struck midnight, then one and two, and still the groups argued and formed opinions. At eighteen minutes after four in the morning, they all straightened up more or less at the same time and directed their gazes to Timothie and his group on the mocha-colored sofa. Soda cans, reams of paper, and coffee cups littered the floor.

A collective sigh arose as a great winged being hovered outside the window, Dareboy on its back. "God bless you and keep you," whispered Uriel, depositing Dareboy gently into the room. Crazy Jack bounced on nimble heels off the hardwood, swished with a noble gesture to the far confines of the room, and grinned in triumph as he held aloft a raft of papers.

"I have their signatures," he announced. "All here. We have elder armies in every country, every state, every province. We flew on enchanted wings to the seven continents of the world. Some countries in the south were the hardest hit. We dealt with corruption, war, fear, and isolationism. But we flew on magic pinions around the world in as little as a few hours. We have consensus. We have the Silver Warriors collective on every continent, every university, every hospital, every school and media outlet. All here." The papers in his hand rustled like so many voices whispering, "Success!"

"What have you done here?" Twirling in his red jumpsuit and leather boots, Dareboy confronted Timothie, his old friend.

"Not so all-inclusive and not so broad as the seven continents of the world, but just the same, a good consensus," Timothie replied.

Ben O'Hara nodded. Ross burped discretely and tucked his double chins into triple, obscuring any signs of a neck. His wife left her group and put her arm around his sloping shoulders. She began to massage the back of his neck. Ross smiled up at her. Ben frowned and grunted.

"We might see for ourselves what the hoopla is about," Timothie offered, opening a box in a corner. Dozens of yellow goggles spilled out. "Thanks to Reginald, we have a surplus of the Millennial Goggles here. Try them on. See what you think. Is there anyone here who hasn't worn them?"

Several seniors raised their hands. They were given goggles.

"I'm almost afraid to let you wear them," Timothie said. "They are addictive and incite a feeling of helplessness over time. Acquiescence," he corrected himself. "Obedience to authority. It's like we're saying, here we are, take us, we're yours. Our brains, our thoughts, our emotions, our guts, all yours."

"They're so beautiful," breathed Ben. "I play Modern Warfare on my PC with 3-D goggles. These are much better than that. Addictive, yes, I can tell they would be." He sat with mouth open and yellow goggles facing Ross, yet lost in his own small world. Ross adjusted his goggles then ripped them off.

"Damn stupid new things," he countered. "An engineer in the factory adjusted them."

Dareboy beamed, bouncing on one booted foot so that the buckles jingled. "That's right! They've been adjusted by engineers, or rather, neuroscientific engineers, who are skilled in marketing. The software automatically updates itself. It's a wonder in engineering."

"There's no escape," grunted Ben. "As a psychologist, I can see the genius of it."

"Thanks for the help you were in overseeing the group process," Timothie said. "I couldn't have done this by myself."

"Of course not. None of us can do all this by ourselves. We need each other. We need the whole world to unite, the world of Silver Warriors, that is. Are they all tuned in to us now? I don't know what Uriel and Dareboy have done." Ben patted his rotund belly and smiled. "I know that we've all had a good night here, though. And look, the sun is coming up."

"More coffee, anyone?" Timothie asked, always the perfect host. He passed out biscuits and honey.

"I'll poach some eggs and make toast," Patricia offered, bouncing up from her spot near her husband, Santiago. "There's bowls of apples and oranges here, too."

Ross raised his hand to take a glass of milk from Jenny. "Ta, mother." He rummaged in a pocket of his plaid flannel shirt for a Scotch mint.

Stiff and sore, many seniors got to their feet and stretched. Little fluffy clouds to the southeast fluttered with a kaleidoscope of peach, pink, and purple streamers from the rising sun. Long slanting rays of light spilled golden like honey onto the parquet floors, and suddenly the long night became day.

Chapter Twenty-Three

"My German friend's grandson, Liam, is sixteen years old and he hacks into computers," shared Maude to Timothie as they nodded together over toast and marmalade. "Kids these days are little geniuses with electronics. Two-year-olds know more about computers than I do. They can download and upload and get rid of viruses. When I was two or three I was making mudpies on Draxxt," she laughed and bit into a dry piece of toast.

Timothie grinned. "Me, too," he said. "But Liam sounds like he could help us, unless he's really ga-ga over the yellow goggles."

"Oh, he is. He loves them and hates them! He loves the game, but I don't think the software affects him like it does the other kids. He knows too much about it. I think he could be an accomplice of the Silver Warriors." She winked.

"Why don't you ask him to come over to the salon after work today? Wednesdays aren't busy. I should be finished by six."

"He's in Grade Ten at Harry Ainley High School. I'm not sure, but I think his last class is at three on Wednesdays." Maude swirled her toast into the broken yolk of the poached egg.

Timothie munched an apple. "That egg looks disgusting. Give him a call and see what he can do. It might be a thrill for him to break the program that's screwing up the entire world."

Maude took a bite of poached egg, which spilled its yellow yolk onto her fork and dripped through the tines. She swallowed. The rest of the group were making their way to the door and down the stairs to the parking lot.

The stout German woman lingered. "Da, I heard what you just said. I have a grandson, da. His name is Liam Hermann, and he's very smart. He doesn't like the yellow goggles. He says they're turning everybody's brain to mush."

Timothie looked up. "So, he's sixteen and he would be interested in working with us?"

"He's a shy boy but has some good friends. I think he would like to ask them to help. One friend is called Carmen. They're about the same age. Liam was sixteen last February."

"My egg is perfect." Maude considered and pushed her plate back. "It's settled then." She picked up her cell phone and thumbed a number. "Here, Hilda, text him. He likes that best, doesn't he? Especially if he's in school or on the bus."

"Liam has his own car. He could pick her up. She doesn't live too far away," the German woman said.

"I don't know how to approach this," Maude said. "Yellow goggles; can you hack into the software? I think that's what I'll say, right out front bold and direct."

"I'd expect no less from you," Timothie mused. He tossed the apple core onto his plate and rose. He stretched. "I wouldn't say that on the Wi-Fi, though. Too risky. Can you meet him in person?"

"We have lunch together once a week." Hilda reached for the phone. "Every Sunday at the manor where we all live. Or most of us. Ross and Jenny live on their own. So do zwie, I would say, others."

"Nice to meet you, darling," Timothie said and hugged the German woman. "I know we were introduced, but my bad, there were so many new faces."

"Morning," and Hilda hugged him back. "We could have the Silver Warriors and the Millennial Militär, couldn't we, Liebling?"

"Hey, that's good. I'm down with that," Timothie exclaimed. "The Millennial Military German style. Or a Panzerdivision. Brilliant."

"Does it really matter?" Maude asked, as Hilda Hermann wrote a name and number on a paper napkin and pushed it toward her. "I think we ought to focus on getting the job done, Timothie."

"Of course. But we need *esprit de corps*. A rallying motto or song."

"Maybe some cheerleaders?" Maude doodled on the paper napkin with a pencil. "You're our leader. Let's hear some pep talks and then get to work."

"Okay, I get it, dear." Timothie sighed. "This won't be an easy task, though, and we're all tired from the night's planning. Everyone else has gone home. I think it's time for me to get a quick nap then go to work."

"I think we've come up with the best idea after the majority has left," Maude said. "I'll volunteer to let them all know about Liam and Carmen and our plan to hijack the software through some form of hacking device. We have to cover our tracks, though. If Ducksworth and Harper ever find out what we're up to, there'll be hell to pay."

"I'm sure they have their ways of silencing us," Timothie agreed. "I wouldn't be surprised if the CIA isn't part of the conspiracy."

"Of course, it is," snapped Maude. "The whole damn world has been seduced by Reginald's game."

Timothie yawned and stretched again. "It's Bael we ought to worry about."

"I think we've shown he can be contained. Uriel is a powerful ally."

"The software originates from TopStrategy Marketing," Timothie said. "That's where we ought to start."

"I don't know how we're going to do it," Maude replied. She rose and followed Timothie into the living room. They began to pick up cups, glasses, and plates from the floor and tables, took the plates into the kitchen and scraped them. A few minutes later she turned the dial on the large Avocado-colored dishwasher, and hot water could be heard swooshing into the interior.

She stood with her hand on one hip and squinted at Timothie. "I know the young kids can hack into anything. They're responsible for many of the viruses and malware that are making their rounds, Timothie. They do it for fun and for the challenge – to make chaos and disrupt business or show disapproval for the establishment, and to show their friends how smart they are. But mostly they want to steal information or money."

"We want to disrupt the goggles business," stated Timothie. "Completely shut it down."

Maude considered. "Then insert our own directions into the game."

"I don't know if we want to do that. It's a possibility. Just shutting down the chatter that's warping people's minds would suit me," Timothie said. "We don't have to replace it with anything."

"A lot of harm might have been done already. We must make sure nothing like it ever occurs again. The population affected will have to be healed."

"That's beyond the scope of a couple of teenagers." Timothie rubbed his temples. His stubbled cheeks shone silver. "It's beyond my abilities, too. What about Reginald? He created the program. He can end it. He can create another program that heals, not destroys."

"The Millennial Goggles preach obedience. Reginald must have had help. He couldn't do that on his own. The neuromarketing science is too advanced for his level of expertise. How did he do it? Any ideas?"

"Only the most influential neuroscientist in the world could have done this," Timothie declared and punched buttons on his Android. "I know someone who could get through to him, too. He lives in Italy."

"The scientist or your friend?"

"Both. My friend is visiting Italy, and the scientist's name is Professor Sergio Pizzolatto. He's written articles regarding the first cryogenic or frozen human brain transplant in the Journal of Developmental Neuroscience. He's also co-recipient of the International Brain Award in 2017. His daughter is also a noted professor, and guess what her specialty is?"

"Not neuromarketing or computers?"

Timothie laughed. "Bingo. Both. His daughter, Doctor Donatella Pizzolatto, is a noted specialist and professor of Advanced Computing Science and Neuromarketing at the Polytechnic University of Milan, the highest-ranking university in Italy and Europe. Her father is professor emeritus at the nearby University of Milan, also considered one of the best in Europe."

"He's retired then?" Maude asked. "Does he have an office there?"

"Oh, yes, and guess again. Who are good friends of his daughter's assistant, who are also good friends of mine?"

"Timothie, cut it out. I don't know that. Oh. Not your friend, Gianni, from England? And Reginald?"

"Right again. They all met in college and have maintained a friendship over the past twenty-five years, long before I met them. Gianni visits her when in Milan. He's also met Donatella."

"I know Gianni and Reginald have known each other for a long time. I didn't know they met in college. Fascinating. Is Gianni not out of the country now?"

"Yes. He's in Rome." The Android in Timothie's muscular hand ticked as he touched the little keypad with his thumbs.

"Fascinating," Maude repeated. She stretched and yawned. "I heard you about the nap, hun. But it's getting too late to nap now, for you. Don't you have to go to work in a couple of hours?"

"This is too important," Timothie replied. "I just canceled my morning appointments. I'll wait for Gianni to get back to me, then I'll sleep until noon and go to the salon after that. We should have an answer by then, and if you don't mind, Maude, you can contact your grandson and Ingrid's grandson and get that set up."

"Yes. If we find out from the Professors how the neuroscience works and the best way to insert a program that heals the damage done, then the kids can do the rest."

"I hope so."

"There's going to be a lot of surprised users all over the world."

"They'll wake up free some morning," Maude said. She rubbed her eyes. "Darn, I need a nap, too."

Timothie pulled down the blinds and hugged his friend.

"Got to sleep," he said. "Thanks so much for all your help, lovely lady."

As Maude pulled the back door shut behind her, on her way to the stairs and the parking lot below, she heard a phone ring and Timothie answer.

The world is a global village, she thought. *The powers of darkness can't completely bury the light. There's always the dawn. There are good people in the world. We've all been cursed but a curse can be lifted, and the light will shine through the cracks until we stand in the glory of a new age.*

THE GLORY OF A NEW AGE, roared a voice. THAT'S WHAT I SAID, TOO.

It was Bael.

Chapter Twenty-Four

"Timothie Hill Hairdressing," answered Timothie, as Maude's figure disappeared behind the door on her way down the stairs. His cell glowed.

Gianni's baritone voice boomed in his ear all the way from Rome. "We draw closer to a mysterious force of nature, I think, little bro. As fellow snowflakes, Ducksworth's people would call us, we have to band together. You have something there with neuroscience and somebody techie to fix the software. The software and its updates, not the game, are the only explanation for what's happening to our friends all over the world. The plug must be pulled, and soon."

"It's not only Ducksworth and Justin Harper's policies," Timothie replied, "It's all over Europe, Asia, Africa, and Australia. Humanity wasn't born for this."

"We are stardust," agreed Gianni. "Hundreds of thousands of years ago, our DNA was brought here from alien worlds."

"We had a noble purpose." Timothie shifted his weight in his khaki low-rise Diesel jeans. He put his thumbs in his pockets. "We still do. It's been corrupted by something so alien and evil that our seeding from the stars is now suspect."

"Originally, Draxxt was seeded from Earth. So, our forebears hoped to spread their DNA over the entire galaxy and beyond. But this must be stopped first," he continued. He cleared his throat. "Do we have a plan, big bro?"

Gianni chuckled. "Sure, I think so, Timothie. I think your plan is just fine. It all depends on Maude now and her techno savvy young friends."

Timothie pulled his hands from his pockets and leaned on the kitchen counter for support. The building swayed. A red plume of smoke erupted outside his third-floor window.

Rat a tat tat!!!!

"Sounds like gunfire or firecrackers here, right outside my door," he cried. He shut down his Android and threw on his cape, which billowed about his manly shoulders in a dark cloud of silver and gold. Springing to the top of the stairs, he flew with one hand on the bannister to the landing below. He thumbed the remote control for his car, and in the carport outside, his red Volvo 123 purred.

"Maude!"

At the bottom of the landing, his elderly friend with the ash blonde hair and the purple starred top panted before a liquid puddle of putrefaction that swirled in thick eddies toward her Nike Air Jordans. So intent was she on her task that she didn't notice Timothie hovering above her in a fury of protection.

"Maude!" he repeated and dashed his hand to the pavement with a flurry of lightning strikes. Thunder boomed from his outstretched fingertips. The rose tattoo on his left bicep swelled with the force of the musculature beneath it. He roared and disappeared feet first into the black maelstrom with the red and white eyeballs, grotesque in the midst of the evil ocean.

Maude pulled a Glock 43 9mm from her Coach bag and fired a volley of shots into the middle of the mess.

"I don't want to hit you, Timothie. Get out of there!"

"Bullets won't hurt this devil from Hell," Timothie burbled as his face broke the surface.

The gold cross on his cape shone like a thousand suns. He caught the bullets in one hand. They splashed harmlessly into the goop. The superhero hairstylist rose with his arms outstretched, the rose tattoos gleaming on his arms, his cape a black star-spangled cloud over the bubbling mass that was Bael. Purple lightning streaked from his fingertips and dotted the small, thick lake below him with fire. Then the gold cross on his cape flamed and sizzled! The black liquid coagulated into a recognizable form. It dripped with venom. Green slime slid from Bael's mouth as the demon grew in stature and might.

"Quick," Timothie gasped. "The holy water!"

Maude's eyebrows shot up and she clapped her hands. She dug into her Coach bag and brought forth a silver bottle with a sippy spout on it. "Holy water." She muttered an incantation over it and crossed herself. Her Nike sneakers were planted in a wide stance at the edge of the mass that was Bael, and she threw the bottle of water to Timothie's outstretched hand. He withdrew the stopper and sprinkled the water onto Bael's monstrous form. He repeated his secret power incantation three times three.

I am God.

I am God.

I am God.

Bael roared. He laughed. The holy water ran down his face and chest. Where it touched, there were huge gaping holes in Bael's corporeal presentation. Maude snapped shut her flip-top Android.

"They're on their way over," she gasped. "Carmen, Hilda's grandson, and another friend."

"How old are the rest of them?" Timothie continued to chant three times three, a different spell now, one that would repel Bael with the new power that poured into the superhero's heart and soul.

"One is only fifteen, and the other two are sixteen. I wish you'd remember that, Timothie."

"Are they virgins?"

Maude snorted. "I don't know. Probably not."

"They have power, as innocents," Timothie said, swirling about Bael's swaying form. A car backfired in front of the old mansion, and a cacophony of teenaged voices erupted from the side of the house as they pelted around to the back where Maude and Timothie kept the demon at bay.

"Liam!" called Maude. "I don't think you should be here, but when we talked to your Oma, she gave us hope. You give the world hope."

"Grandma told me all about it," the young boy replied, wiping his ginger hair back from his broad forehead. His green eyes glinted. "I have the thumb drive with the program we developed last night." His two friends gaped when they saw the swaying figure of Bael and Timothie and Maude kitty-corner and standing in the stench.

Timothie gritted his teeth. "Great. Now stand back. I don't want any of you hurt."

"Don't worry, dear," Maude said. "I won't let anything harm you. You're out of harm's way as long as you're with my friend Timothie."

"Innocents," gasped Bael and reached out a mighty hand. Liam and his two friends joined hands and stood in a circle. Overhead, thunder cracked. Lightning smashed. A funnel cloud formed to the east. They were pushed back by a blast of wind, and another crack of thunder heralded a deluge of hail.

Bael groaned.

"I am God. I am God. I am God," intoned Timothie. The day was dark as midnight when Uriel rocked their world with a majestic voice that sounded like thunder. With a white pinioned wing and ivory arms, she embraced Timothie and they became one.

The pavement opened up. Bael screamed. A white iridescence glowed like a nuclear explosion in the midst of the parking lot behind the gracious old mansion. Maude swayed in the whirlwind that ensued, her mouth open, her eyes wide and sparkling, and Liam and his friends embraced her, too. Her Glock clattered to the pavement.

"That's illegal, Maude," Liam cried "This isn't Arizona."

"And I'm not Jesse James," agreed Maude and grinned. Where Bael had towered only moments before there was nothing but an oil slick on the pavement and a smell of burning tar. They all turned their eyes away from the glory that was Timothie and his Angel.

"Liam," Maude said. "Let's see that thumb drive."

"Sure, Mrs. Maude," the boy replied. He held out his hand.

A great golden presence separated from their friend Timothie Hill, and the voice of Uriel whispered, "It's almost over. The demons of Hell are near to harvesting six billion souls for the last great war with the Heavens. God's throne was never in danger. But we must fight the good battle, for the soldiers of Heaven are preparing for the onslaught that was prophesied. Not a word must be taken from the prophesy or there will be a curse on he or she who removes it."

"That would be me," said Timothie and grinned.

"Is this Armageddon?" asked Maude.

"No," said the Angel. "But it might mean the end of the world as you know it. The end of one of the ages."

"That's okay," Liam said and tossed the thumb drive to his grandmother's friend. She caught it as it flashed through the air and put it in the hip pocket of her Wrangler boyfriend jeans. "We had nothing else to do this week," he continued. "Might as well – erm – save the world."

"Don't be proud," Maude cautioned. "Pride comes before a fall."

"Can we go home now?" asked Liam's brown-faced friend with the gorgeous straight black hair and the lip ring. "This is bad shite here." He glanced about him nervously. Carmen and the boys had stopped holding hands and broken the circle.

Timothie smiled. "I think your part isn't done. We need help with breaking the software, like your Oma said. We need young people, precision, and knowledge. You would be available, your grandmother said. She said you're all hackers, laugh out loud. Thanks, guys. Couldn't have done this without you. But can you help us with the program?"

"Awesome," the First Nations boy muttered.

"We'll keep you in mind," Carmen said.

"How much do we get?" asked Liam. He winked and rubbed his hands together.

In a rush of air, Uriel departed. Hail bounced off the tarmac and collected in piles on the side of the building.

"If you write about this someday, Timothie," called Maude. "Don't mention the weather. Agents hate that."

Timothie slapped his hand onto his muscular thigh. "I wouldn't dream of it," he said. "Maude, my friend, you were on your way home. Is your old Mercedes still driveable or should I offer you a ride in the Volvo? We can fly. I can hear it purring in the carport now."

"Actually, my car is fine. It might sprout wings itself, who knows? Stranger things have happened today."

"Hey, kids," called Timothie. "I'll give you two hundred each."

Done!" called Carmen and Liam together, and the other boy shrugged. "Okay."

Chapter Twenty-Five

"Selling to the old brain for instant success. To win the battle we sell to the soul. The seat of the self, not the new brain that's been overlaid by evolution, but the old brain that really controls their actions and beliefs," boasted Reginald Smith.

He hesitated; the man behind the huge curved desk chuckled. The wide room in the Oval Office in Washington, D.C., whispered echoes of his voice at four o'clock in the morning. Images of Lincoln and Washington watched benignly from the walls. The desk was devoid of anything but gleaming electronics, an eagle icon, and an untidy pile of papers.

Three large south-facing windows behind the President's desk were draped in somber burgundy velvet. A fireplace burned on the north side. Four doors on each side of the oval opened onto the Rose Garden, the office of the President's secretary, the President's study and dining room, and the remaining door opened onto the corridor of the West Wing. Three Secret Service agents huddled beside the fireplace, weapons drawn.

Reginald scribbled a diagram on a notepad and slid it across the desk to the man in front of him. "Here it is," he said. "The answer to neuromarketing. See, there's the unconscious mind – the old brain – and the conscious or rational mind, the new brain. The Millennial Goggles go deep within the old brain from where our actions and beliefs actually spring. Our thinking mind, or frontal lobes, are a fairly recent development in evolutionary terms. We might think we make rational decisions, but actually that's not true. The unconscious mind controls your citizens, sir, the old brain controls the world.

"Neuromarketers and politicians and corporations know this, though they might not know the mechanisms exactly, but they know how to manipulate it. What I've done? Simply put the goals and rewards neatly into this package that appeals to the old brain so precisely that your citizens are helpless against it. The dopamine factor, the pleasure factor, hooks them, and then the neurosensors embedded in the goggles wend deep within their unconscious brains and poof – they're your puppets."

"How'd you come up with them, Reginald?" The large man rose and paced like a panther.

"I was approached by my company to devote an entire department to their development." Reginald cleared his throat and stroked his thin mustache with his index finger. "On your orders, sir. Our P.M. also authorized it, but I wasn't aware of it at the time. Of course, they're demonic..." he whispered the rest and the large man leaned over to hear him. "It's odd to see you without your tie, sir. Are you golfing today?"

"Absolutely not. I absolutely am not golfing today. I agreed to meet you with only my trusted advisors present." The shadowy figures standing at the north side of the room stirred and one of them coughed. "I absolutely do not wear a tie twenty-four seven. There is no one more informal than me or humbler when meeting with international figures. Nobody humbler. I am absolutely the humblest. You can depend on that."

"Thank you, Mr. President," Reginald murmured and drew another quick diagram on the yellow foolscap pad. "You'll see here where the very smallest bundles of energy from the goggles are converted into brain waves on the unconscious level. Vivid images, very pleasant experiences, interactive games with a rush of pleasure unknown to opiates or heroin, but similar, and very addictive. The manipulation of memories to our advantage. It's basically a memory neurotransmitter covered by a fantastic game that infiltrates the old brain which has been developing for millions of years. They can't resist it. They're helpless in its simplistic power, but the complexity of the images fools them into following the impulses right down the rabbit hole."

"I don't believe we've been evolving for millions of years," Dennis Ducksworth snorted. "The Earth is only eight thousand years old. My trusted advisors have told me as much. Is this *science*, Mr. Smith? I absolutely do not believe in science. My citizens are animals? Is that what you're telling me?" Reginald heard the safety click on a gun from the corner where the Secret Service agents hovered.

"Well, Mr. President. May I call you Dennis?"

"I am absolutely the humblest. But you may not call me Dennis. No, absolutely not. I hired you to do this simple thing, and it appears it works. That's all. That's all I wanted to know. But what are you telling me about this science thing? You're not a scientist, Reginald. I certainly am not. I am certainly not a scientist. Is that what you're telling me?"

Reginald frowned. It was best to be cautious in his approach. He noticed a wisp of smoke curl around a corner of the desk. An edge of the carpet burned. He thought furiously, *Bael, get lost. This isn't the time.*

"We all know this is not exactly science the way it began, Mr. President, your honor. It began as a pact between myself and er…"

"Yes, yes. The dark forces you spoke of. I don't, of course, believe a word of it. I will work for the citizens of America. I love America. It is my wish to make it the greatest nation on Earth. These goggles will bring all other countries to their knees, waiting for America to lead them. To lead them out of the swamp of their own stupidity, believing in old brains and new brains and the Devil's idea of evolution. I don't believe that. Absolutely not. But the goggles work, Reginald." He strode around the desk and threw an arm over Reginald's shoulders, knocking Reginald's glasses askew. Reginald straightened his lenses and picked up a thumb drive. He inserted it into the goggles.

"This might be unnecessary," he said. "The goggles are self-replicating, self-perpetuating, never in need of power. But when I insert this thumb drive – poof! All the information that was a memory to the guy who wore them, friggin' – excuse me, sir – but friggin' transformed to waves of light that travel from a fifth dimension to the far reaches of the Earth. And all other goggles are attuned to the vibrations that are in this master set; we can change their message in an instant. I've been working to improve this program. This is Delta Two. Me and my staff have named it that because it's carried on Delta waves that kick in when the citizen is sleeping."

"Ah. Ingenuous."

"That would be ingenious, sir."

"Yes, yes, whatever. I absolutely know that. But what are you saying now, guy? We've gone on to the next step? We have the world completely under our control, and now we're on to Step Two? Where they're under the thumb of the greatest country in the world?"

"More than that," murmured Reginald. The carpet smoked. He fidgeted and sat heavily in the leather chair in front of the gleaming desk. The President picked up the goggles once more.

"These are the master goggles?"

"You could call them that. Actually, any pair could be the master goggles once the thumb drive with my new program is inserted. We've done it, sir. While the world sleeps, the neuromemories will erase their former selves, and they'll be entirely doing your bidding and the bidding of your neighboring country. Peace will prevail on Earth."

"It's the only way we could guarantee peace," murmured Dennis Ducksworth. "To stop the wars around the globe, to stop the anti-creationists and the Godless, we must threaten nuclear war and ensure that we are the only country that holds the power. The power to bring peace."

"Exactly, Mr. President." Reginald grinned. A form wavered in the corner of the dimly lit room. The Secret Service agents moaned. "They're affected, too," Reginald pointed out.

The President grunted. "I don't want to know what's behind it. Keep that demon out of here, Mr. Smith."

"I don't know if I can. A deal is a deal," Reginald said. But the ethereal form in the corner flickered and disappeared. The three Secret Service agents moved forward.

"This is the night. As soon as the world goes to sleep, all over the globe, one by one the lights go out. They'll wake up in the morning with peace and obedience in their hearts as soon as they put the goggles back on. It's inexorable. It's complete and appeals to the most primitive part of their brains, that which really controls their decisions."

"Peace and obedience in their hearts or their minds? Absolutely doesn't make a difference. Reginald, you're a genius."

"I had help," Reginald admitted as the carpet smoked. "I think this program can't be broken. But there is someone with friends…"

"What do you mean?"

"Oh, nothing," he said, his words spilling out of his pursed lips without thought. "Just a friend of mine seems suspicious. It's probably nothing."

"What friends?"

"I shouldn't have mentioned it. His name is Timothie, and he lives in Edmonton, Alberta."

"Where's that?"

"Canada, sir. A western province."

The President pursed his lips. "Is he a threat?"

"I don't think so. But he's a force to be reckoned with."

"I'll put my tracers on him. He has a cell phone?"

"This is his number," Reginald said.

"Good enough. He's some kind of scientist, too?"

Reginald shifted his weight in the chair. "I shouldn't have mentioned it, sir. I'm sure it's nothing. No, he's not a scientist. He's a hairdresser."

"Hmmm. Good. Good, Reginald." The President slapped the blond man on his back. "A hairdresser is privy to a lot of talk. A lot of gossip. Has a lot of news. A lot of information. Is this a smart man, then, my friend?"

"Oh, yes. Very. I think he would be a real adversary if he knew what I know."

"He still thinks you're his friend?"

"I think so," Reginald confirmed. "I think he believes I'm his friend. He invites me to his parties."

"Are they good parties?" Dennis Ducksworth put his head in his hands and closed his eyes. "Would he have a lot of friends?"

"Oh, yes."

"Anybody else you know who'd interfere with the peace we're proposing?"

"No. Pretty well everyone I can find out about is addicted to the yellow goggles. To the Millennial Goggles, as they call it. Only a few seem immune."

"We'll fix them."

All over the world, vibrations from the fifth dimension entered the synapses of the instruments which carried the unconscious of the citizens of the world. Peace would reign under the benevolent rule of the United States of America and its President.

Only one man stood in the way. Timothie Hill.

Chapter Twenty-Six

Justin Harper, Prime Minister of Canada – dapper, grey-haired, in his early sixties, and impeccably dressed in a pink shirt, burgundy tie, and white suit – whipped out his tablet from under one muscular arm and laughed aloud. He adjusted his yellow goggles over shell-like ears. Power fascinated him, not the money he had been born to, but the snake of power that gripped him now around his throat and strangled any sense of morality or concern for the citizens of his country. His mentor, Dennis Ducksworth, sent three succinct words in a message to Justin: *It is done.*

Colors kaleidoscoped behind the lenses of his Millennial Goggles, cascading in unheard of patterns from the fifth dimension and even more, from that region of space/time that was controlled by entities too terrible and powerful to be encompassed in rational thought. The games they presented were more addictive than heroin, as the brain struggled and leaped to complete the sequences that piled evermore in pillars of thought and emotion from the master program. Behind the concept of a simple game which the world had adopted as its own existed the chilling possibility of a wormlike intrusion into the unconscious mind, setting up repetitive cycles of memory and synapses that didn't exist in nature.

Justin stopped to scan the headlines from CBC on his tablet. There it was; the threat from the U.S.A. of nuclear war – a posturing in the Indian Ocean, troops allocated to the Sudan, long-range missiles targeting North Korea, Egypt under siege by the CIA, the Middle East a supernova of intrigue, bloodshed, and murder. Under the threat of involvement and retaliation by the greatest nation on Earth simmered the seductive hiss of the Millennial Goggles: Peace.

Wet-hot American rhetoric blanketed the promise that the world awoke to that morning. *Do not resist. Salvation is at hand. Give us your souls, give us your hearts and unconscious minds, sink to the undersurface of anything you once knew as progress, and obey your Masters.*

Because we will take your souls.

Justin laughed again, unable to stop chuckling, slapped his hand on his muscular thigh, and smirked. He held a double double Tim Horton's coffee in his right hand and slipped the tablet into his briefcase with his left hand.

President Ducksworth had promised him a share of the yellow gold that poured from the Earth's coffers into oil, war machines, and clean water. It would all be theirs, but more than that, Justin Harper knew the creature behind this blessing of peace, and it wasn't a blessing at all, he thought, it was a curse. No one knew that but the elite few.

They would sell their souls to the Devil for a piece of the yellow gold, but for him, it was for power. Canada and Mexico together would become the second greatest nations on Earth. India and China must be defeated. Even now, millions on millions of Chinese and Indian nationals wore the goggles and awoke to the concept of benevolence and humility. They dropped their technological superiority as their old brains kicked in with a dopamine rush more powerful than heroin. *Obey*, they intoned and called in absent to their myriad offices, corporations, institutions, hospitals, schools, and warehouses. Office towers stood empty. Computers whined unattended.

Justin's eyes glazed. His gleaming wing-tipped shoes whispered across the tiled floors of the Commons. "We'll have peace in our day."

He murmured "Good morning" to his assistant and entered his office. The paneled walls reflected his image. He smoothed his grey collar-length hair and tossed his briefcase onto the polished surface of his huge cherry wood credenza.

His assistant, Ms. Esther Pleasantview, tapped on his door and fluttered in with a tray of scones and fruit. His inbox was neatly catalogued, and files were piled in alphabetical order by the antique desk clock his staff had given him the year before for his sixty-first birthday.

He dismissed the scones with a wave of his hand and Esther fluttered out again. He sipped on his double double. He couldn't help but notice that Ms. Pleasantview wore her yellow goggles and seemed less sure of herself this morning than usual. The scones and fruit, too, took the place of the correspondence she usually presented first thing in the morning. Something had changed.

Justin tapped a message to his counterpart in Washington. *What now, Dennis?*

His phone was quiet this morning. No urgent calls, no meetings marked off on his calendar, no RCMP officers intruding on his day, though he knew that two stood guard outside his door. At least he *thought* they did. He got up and opened the heavy door, peeked out into the hallway, and saw some officers standing in the corridor wearing yellow goggles and smirking.

"What's the joke?" he asked. They responded with the Peace sign, fingers apart, and from down the long empty corridor came the sound of a single speaker addressing the House of Commons.

"We're alone," he heard the speaker say, and then there was silence. The officers nodded and grinned, then one by one, adjusting their goggles, sauntered down the corridor toward the exit. A lone guard stood erect near his door. He recognized someone from CSIS, the Canadian Security Intelligence Service, collide with the RCMP officers in his hurry to exit the building. Justin stepped back inside his office and closed the door.

"Yes, things have changed," he said to Esther. "Would you like to go home this morning, Ms. Pleasantview? There seems very little to do here this morning."

"Why no, sir," she said, and her cheeks turned as rosy as the dawn. "There's no one at home to miss me."

"I have a beautiful wife and four children," commented Justin. "But I won't be going home this morning, nor will I meet Sophia for lunch as we planned. Please give her a call, Esther. It seems to me that something momentous has taken place today." He adjusted his goggles. Soothing yet discordant images assaulted his senses. He struggled to slot the brilliant rainbows of his mind into the correct categories and to win the game, or at least to play it as best he could, but the message came through from a subterranean level of his consciousness: *Peace.*

If not peace, what then? he thought. Riding a nuclear bomb to oblivion, opening a box that blew away part of his head and all of the buildings on Parliament Hill? A bullet in the gut, a firestorm in one's home, a shower of radioactive death in particles from nuclear explosions that made Hiroshima look like the Fourth of July? What was the alternative to peace?

He sipped on his Tim Horton's coffee and smiled, following the patterns in his conscious brain, the patterns that, like a snake, wormed into the entrails of everything that meant anything to him in his unconscious mind. His childhood flashed past the crimson lenses. He knew he loved his wife, his children, his parents, his friends, but a strange sudden indifference tempered that love. Nothing seemed to mean anything more than the worm that was in his old brain, burrowing past mindfulness. *Peace.*

Dennis Ducksworth was right. Peace was all that mattered, under the benevolent eye of a demon.

Had he thought that? Where had that thought come from? The door opened and closed. His assistant leaned in front of him, looking dim and faraway, smiling. Her yellow-rimmed goggles with the crimson lenses reflected the glow of the artificial fireplace behind his desk.

"May I go home now, sir? I don't feel well."

"Of course," he answered. "I think we should all go home."

"No, there's business to be done this afternoon," she said. "It's important. The Egyptian ambassador had an appointment at ten, but he's canceled. You've had back to back meetings all day, and every one of them has canceled or rescheduled. Yet I think it's an important day. It's urgent you be here. You know what I mean." He saw her wink behind the lenses.

"Yes," he replied. "Send in the U.S. Ambassador."

"Exactly. He's been waiting in the anteroom with his aides."

Justin dismissed his assistant and strode into the next room where the U.S. Ambassador, Bruce Wilkins Kraft, waited with two of his trusted assistants.

"Wait here," Bruce said to his companions and followed Justin into the next room. "I guess you know what happened," he continued as they seated themselves at the long rectangular Board table.

"No," Justin said and smiled again. He sipped on a glass of spring water that Esther had put out for him and poured some for Ambassador Kraft from a crystal pitcher. "Tell me."

He relaxed. He threw his long legs under the table and stretched his arms above his head. Images flashed into the back of his brain. He tossed the yellow goggles onto the gleaming chrome tabletop and turned toward the U.S. Ambassador, who did the same.

"Life is good," Justin commented. "And Canada will be great, not for the first time."

"Really?" Ambassador Kraft coughed. "You have consulted with President Ducksworth, then."

"Of course not." Justin toyed with his glass. He glanced at his mobile on the table set to vibrate. His home number appeared on the screen. Sophia had called. He could hear the landline in his assistant's office shrilling. No one was there to answer.

"I've canceled all my appointments for today. Except for you," Justin continued. "It isn't as important as you may think, though. Not as important as going home right now, Bruce. Just a message for your boss."

"Which is?"

Justin flashed his fingers in the Peace sign. "You know Canada's motto? *A Mari usque ad Mare.*"

"So?" Ambassador Kraft sipped at his water. He put down the glass. He wiped his forehead, which beaded with sweat.

"It comes from Psalm 72 verse 8 in the King James Bible, which reads in Latin: *Et dominabitur a mari usque ad mare, et a flumine usque ad terminos terrae.*"

"So, what shall I tell President Ducksworth?"

"Canada will eclipse his little posturing. 'He shall have dominion also from sea to sea, and from the river unto the ends of the Earth.' "

"Interesting," the ambassador said. "But statistics say you're wrong, little man."

The Prime Minister swirled patterns onto the chrome of the tabletop. "I don't think so. Tell Ducksworth the goggles are ours. They were invented by a Canadian, and a Canadian has programmed them. I've made sure that Mr. Smith patented the goggles, and he controls that which is behind the worldwide phenomenon."

"You're not saying you control Reginald Smith, are you, Justin?"

"Yes," he said. "That's the message I want you to convey to the President. We control the goggles because we control Mr. Smith."

"We weren't aware of that."

"How does it feel to be a second-class country? Soon to be third world."

The ambassador snorted. "That's ridiculous."

"Is it?" Justin swung one impeccably shod foot over an impeccably clad knee. "I've always wondered what drove Ducksworth. I think it's not money. He has enough. I think, like me, it's power."

"Power drives all powerful men."

"It also has its price."

"Yes." The ambassador perspired. "This room is hot." He wiped his brow with a blindingly white handkerchief.

"We like it that way. Canada's been on the hot seat too long. It's our turn, Bruce."

"I don't know what you mean."

Justin smiled. "We've been a mouse sleeping with an elephant too long. Every time the elephant turns over in bed, the mouse gets crushed."

"That's the nature of politics. And rather untrue, my friend."

"No, it's true. Until now." Justin put his long legs under the chair and got up. The U.S. Ambassador also rose. "We shall have dominion also from sea to sea, and from the river unto the ends of the Earth."

"Is that the message you want me to give the President? Rather cheeky, I'd say."

"Yes. And you can tell him I talked to Bael."

"Bael?" The ambassador wiped his brow again. He blinked. A corner of the room smoked, and the fireplace roared to life. Inside the flames, he heard burbling laughter that seemed to come all the way from Hell.

"Yes. Onto the ends of the Earth. He wants your souls, you know. I think that's a small price to pay for power. Why, I don't even believe in the next world, old man. If you believe you have a soul, you should worry. Because this is the end of the world."

The ambassador rushed out of the room.

"Tell Dennis," called Justin after him. "Tell him I said Reginald is mine."

The ambassador squealed over his shoulder, "Go to Hell!"

Justin laughed. Life was good.

Chapter Twenty-Seven

The Silver Warriors once again assembled, but this time with only Maude, Timothie, and, surprisingly, Reginald Smith. A dark form stirred ever-present in the corner but didn't make itself visible, and over the mantle of the portable brick fireplace hovered a great being with wings of snow white. The three humans huddled over a table in the dining area, empty except for a box of yellow goggles, a pad of paper and pens, and a small thumb drive.

"Their power comes from the inside out," explained Reginald, fondling a pair of goggles. Neural connectors sparkled along the inside of the plastic arms. "Their message is bonded to fundamental archetypes common to all humans. When an input is made from a distance, as happened today all over the globe in different time zones, the wearers are helpless to avoid the impulses that vibrate in a common harmony from a source that so far is a secret."

Maude rubbed the side of her face and frowned. "What's the purpose?"

"To capture a soul," Timothie whispered. "Here are the coordinates of the quantum computer you used to create the logarithms."

"It's hidden deep inside the university," Reginald said. "They used information from the atom smasher at Geneva, Switzerland. The Millennial Goggles use quarks and other subatomic particles, whirling from hyperspace in the fantastic images we see, to penetrate the brain's amygdala, which governs emotions, survival instincts, and memory."

Maude scribbled on the pad of paper. "Can it wipe out memory? Create false emotions and false memories, threaten or stimulate fear?"

"All of those," Reginald replied. "What happened this morning was not a coincidence. We planned it from the beginning. All the nations of the world live in fear of the loss of peace, their memories of evil wiped out and replaced with images of benevolent dictators, their emotions flattened and ready to receive orders from their savior."

"Bael?" Timothie guessed. "In the guise of President Ducksworth?"

"Actually, no." Reginald removed his eyeglasses and placed the goggles on his face. He smiled. Dreams began to carouse about his head in an almost palpable form.

Timothie looked on, appalled, put on a pair of the goggles himself, and experienced the same emotions, the same memories, the same thoughts as billions of people the world over. Universal world order had almost been achieved. Almost. Timothie ripped off the goggles. Reginald hummed to himself and threw his goggles across the table.

"Why now?" Maude asked again. "Why do you come to help us now, Reginald? Keeping your enemies close isn't your forte."

Something huge moaned and stirred in a dark corner. Reginald's eyes widened, and his mouth formed an "O." Timothie reached across the table and patted his former friend on the back.

"He's come to his senses," the hairstylist murmured, biceps straining against the sleeveless dress shirt he wore. "After what happened this morning, all over the world, due to your manipulations, Reg – you're afraid, aren't you? You are, after all, a member of the human race."

Reginald nodded and swallowed. "I've made a big mistake. Turn on the news. See for yourself."

The superhero switched the Roku to CBC news, and the face of a familiar announcer appeared instantly.

The announcer's face was stern, and his eyes displayed deep concern. Behind him were images of street scenes in Europe and the Middle East, people crowding about shop windows staring at the merchandise, eyes vacant. As the scene flashed to Moscow, hordes of citizens in Red Square chanted and Russian soldiers waved MP-443 Grach sidearms over their heads to the tune of the Russian military song, *On Guard for Peace.* Perspiration beaded on Reginald's forehead. He wiped his face with a folded Canada bandanna.

"See that?" he said. Timothie shrugged.

"Looks good to me. They're talking peace."

Maude peered closer, her blue eyes sharp. "At what price?"

"Change the channel," urged Reginald. Similar scenes flashed by as Timothie's fingers tapped the remote, then settled on a scene from the isolated African country of Eparitrea. There, President Abimbola Patrick held a huge black microphone in a pink-palmed fist and roared in Arabic and English his resolution of unity for the world.

"What's this all about?" asked Timothie. "I've never heard of this country."

Reginald's mouth thinned to a pink line under his mustache. "You will."

Over the mantel, Uriel spread her snowy wings to encompass the entire north wall of Timothie's living area. She moaned, a cathedral-like tone sounding like pipe organs and Bach. Timothie looked down. Cutworms covered the floor, thick and squirming, juicy in their shuddering mass. Reginald screamed and whipped his feet to the rungs of his chair.

"Lepidoptera!" Maude cried and pounded her booted foot into the squirming crush.

Timothie's navy Converse sneakers twitched but held firm on the floor beneath his plastic ghost chair. He reached across the expanse of worms to his gym bag and pulled out his spangled black and silver cape. The gold cross emblazoned on the back gleamed and flashed.

Reginald produced a small vial of holy water from his blazer pocket and threw it into the dark corner from which the worms appeared to originate. Something there, huge and viscous, groaned and laughed. Uriel's voice grew stronger. From the heavens to the south of the apartment, through the open windows from the dank air outside, came a celestial sighing of a multitude of holy spirits. Timothie hovered a foot above the roiling heap of cutworms, which had begun to climb the furniture.

"We must be on to something," he said, "or this wouldn't be happening. Maude, insert the thumb drive into that pair of goggles that Reg threw across the table."

Reginald nodded. "I believe any pair of goggles can be the master goggles."

A mob surrounded the President of Eparitrea, chanting and saluting, some bowing, while he stood on a podium high above the crowd and waved a pair of Millennial Goggles. First, he shouted in Arabic, then in the other eight languages of his country, including English. Timothie caught the words, *God's will* and *surrender to me* and *a new world order.* In the background, soldiers in military uniforms drove huge trucks with what appeared to be intercontinental missiles riding on their backs.

"Abimbola Patrick, the new self-proclaimed savior of the world; can anything good come out of Eparitrea, the North Korea of Africa?" asked Reginald as the holy water hissed and burned into a fearsome figure that flickered and then faded in the far corner. Worms stank and sizzled where the water had splashed onto the floor.

Timothie reached across the table and helped Maude to insert the thumb drive into the proper outlet on Reginald's goggles. The worms squirmed up the furniture and began to cover the table. Maude brushed them off and peered at the goggles more closely, her eyes next to the interface that appeared on the underside of the device.

"What now?" she asked.

"I don't know." Timothie still hovered above the floor. He whirled and grasped the goggles in his muscular yet gentle hand.

"I don't know what Liam and his friends did to the program," Maude said. "We should maybe ask him to come over."

"With this mess?" Timothie gestured at the dark corner from where the worms spilled in steaming masses.

"Oh, that," Maude whispered. "Reg? Can you help us?"

Reginald snorted. "You're on your own."

"Whose side are you on?" Timothie asked suspiciously. He spread his cloak, and it grew, overlapping black on black, silver stars across a golden cross. The magical fabric flashed and settled across the floor as the cutworms *screamed* and Uriel roared a blessing. Crimson flames burned the moth larvae to cinders. Nothing remained but a dusting of ash and a terrible stench in the room.

"I'll have to clean this," Timothie murmured and picked up his cloak. Reginald sat thin-lipped on the other side of the table. "You can't be trusted. We all knew that, Reg," Timothie continued.

"I didn't do friggin' nothing," Reginald whined. He toyed with another pair of yellow goggles. "That program you have isn't working, dude. What's it supposed to do?"

"It's supposed to negate the curse that was put on the world this morning when we all woke up to a populace that worships Bael," Maude said. She tapped her foot. "A world of people that won't help themselves, that serve Peace rather than Progress."

"Isn't that a good thing?"

"It would be if peace weren't gained at the expense of their souls." Timothie whipped his cloak onto the table and sat again on the transparent ghost chair. "Thanks for the holy water. It seems to contain the demon somewhat. But not good enough. I presume you carried it for your own protection, and you're getting scared, old friend? What have you unleashed into the world, you and your Millennial Goggles? Was it what you expected to happen?"

"No," Reginald said. He cupped his stubbled face in his hands, his long blond hair falling over his greasy forehead. "I have a confession. I subverted the President of the United States. He thinks he's the new savior. But he's not. It's Abimbola from Eparitrea, and they have nuclear power. He holds absolute sway over an unstable country, and Bael loves him; he's the host.

"Really. It's not Ducksworth or Harper, the likely suspects in our western world. It's somebody from a remote corner of the world, an isolated country, yet powerful beyond measure as the scriptures of the Book of the Dead indicate. Can anything great come from the continent that's been so abused for so many centuries by God's nations?"

"Yes," breathed Maude. "Good will always overcome evil."

"If it does," Reginald replied, "then I've picked the right side at last."

"Call Liam," Timothie urged. He fixed Maude with a meaningful gaze. "Ask him and his two clever friends to come over here. I'll go pick them up if necessary. You have the number, Maude. He has to tweak this program they've come up with. I'm not sure the kids knew the full range of what's on the Millennial Goggles or know the extent of the neuroscience that's gone into them. I suspect the images are from another dimension, maybe something created by the accelerator in Geneva that hasn't been discovered yet, and put together by Reginald, not so clever Reg, but with the help of a demon from Hell."

"Who knows everything." Reginald grinned and got up. He swaggered toward the door, the box of goggles under his arm. "You can keep the master goggles. I have plenty more where those came from."

As the door slammed shut, Timothie leaned across the table to Maude, who scribbled furiously on her pad of paper. "He's sitting on the fence," he whispered. "We know we can't trust him. He's hoping if Bael wins and the world bows to a peace orchestrated by Eparitrea, then the six billion souls of Earth will be delivered to Hell to fight for God's throne."

"They won't win, of course," Maude said, putting down her pen and tapping a number on her mobile phone. "Liam? You answered on the second ring. You knew it was me?"

"Yes," she said, after a pause. "You may pick up the other two." She listened for a moment more, then flipped her phone shut. "He's coming right away, with the others. He might need the extra help."

"No problem," Timothie replied. "The Volvo will fly, you know. Much faster."

"Might scare the Josephat out of him. And as for Reg – no, Bael won't win the throne of God, but it will be Armageddon, and all those billions of souls will be lost if they fight on the side of Satan."

Timothie pulled his lower lip with two fingers. "Who's to say they won't win?"

"Exactly," Maude said. "We don't know that, do we?"

"My customer, Starr, knows something. I wonder what? Or maybe Bael usurps all my friends, my clients, my family…"

"Starr with her psychedelic locks? She suspects, that's all. She thinks she's psychic, Timothie. I know her well, through Julie Ann Carter, who knows a lot of people. Julie Ann makes friends with everyone."

"She's a sweetheart. But Starr worries me. So do you. You both know too much about the dark force, and that isn't good."

"It may be good for you, to help you out, Timothie, have you thought of that? We're here to help you, not to bring you down."

"I love you, Maude."

"We hope to win, but it isn't reality, really, Timothie, that good always wins. You know that by looking at the news or hearing about the latest tragedy. There's a huge battle to be waged yet. We sometimes only have hope. Hope is all we have."

Uriel, forgotten over the mantel, moaned and stirred her great white wings, enveloped the room with love, then whispered into invisibility.

"I think you're right," Timothie agreed. "Hope and Armageddon."

Chapter Twenty-Eight

"Time to call in the troops, is it, Maude?" asked Liam, sauntering through the doorway of Timothie's apartment condo, thumbs in the pockets of his low-slung jeans. "Couldn't you figure it out without us, dude?"

His brown-faced friend with the gorgeous straight black hair grinned and flicked two fingers in a salute of "Peace" or perhaps "Victory." He reached out a pale hand to grasp the thumb drive on Timothie's table.

"Give us a minute," he said. The master goggles lay on the table beside the miniature drive.

"Dude," Liam began, his red hair gleaming beneath the overhead lamps, "it might take three of us to figure it out, but I doubt it. I think I know where we went wrong in the first place. Here..."

He inserted the drive into the USB slot in the goggles. Immediately a green light flashed and pulsed. Liam settled the goggles onto his face. He peered at the room with his green eyes through ruby tinted lenses. "Hmmm..." he said. "You're right. It's not uploading properly, but some of it is there."

"Let me try," said the brown-faced fellow. Liam passed the goggles to his friend.

"Can you do any better, James?" he asked. The other boy squinted and adjusted some buttons on the inside of the goggles.

"Let me have my cell," James said. "I'll tell you in a minute what we should do."

Carmen pulled on a strand of long blonde hair self-consciously. "I think I've got it," she said and thumbed her iPad. "It's all here. We've got Wi-Fi and the thumb drive is streaming. It's uploading like it should, man. The problem is in the goggles. The program that's in there is password protected and has a firewall."

"Pretty sophisticated stuff for a pair of eyeglasses," James said and consulted his own phone. "You're right, Carmen. We have to crack the code."

"That's easy," ventured the pale girl. "Let's all three of us sit down across the table and do this thing, man."

"I've got a code-cracking program on my iPad," bragged James, tucking his Fuse tee-shirt into his low-slung jeans. "We do this all the time, don't we, guys? Cracked the code to the RNIB Bank a couple years ago when we were starting out. Did a lot of havoc, too, and that was only the beginning of our genius."

"Yeah, we're friggin' geniuses," agreed Liam. "Let us at it, man."

All three sat across Timothie's dining room table, and their thumbs flew on the small keyboards. Blue lights flashed. They peered at the screens, groaned, and slapped the table.

"How about a pop, Timothie?"

"Sure," Timothie agreed, strode to the kitchen and extracted three Dr. Peppers from the refrigerator. "Here, is this okay?"

"Sure."

"Dear, would you like a snack?" asked Maude, running her gnarly fingers through her ash blonde pixie cut. She brought out cold cuts, cheese, and big slabs of toast with mustard and mayo.

"Thanks, Mrs. Maude," Liam said, frowning at the screen. His companions began to scribble logarithms on a pad of paper by their elbows.

"Bingo!" Carmen cried. "I think I've got it!"

A musical note emanated from the Millennial Goggles, and a blue light flashed intermittently, illuminating the faces of the three friends hunched over their tablets and cell phones.

"Right on," Timothie murmured. He leaned over the shoulders of Carmen's two companions. "Can you upload the program now?"

"I don't know," James said, his brown face wrinkled with concentration and perspiration beaded his forehead. "It's awful hot in here, Timothie."

Indeed, all five humans were covered in sweat. The overhead lamp glowed blue-white. The fireplace was cold. Curtains hung cheerily over the dark windows. "It's been a warm day," Timothie acknowledged and turned on a couple of tower fans. "Is that better?"

"Sort of. I don't know why it should be so darn hot." James wiped his forehead with the back of a dark hand. "Wait."

"What?" Timothie held his breath. Maude squealed with excitement. She built a tall sandwich from the fixings and shoved half of it in Liam's direction. "Eat this, dear. You need to keep up your strength. You've been at this for hours."

"No thanks," Liam muttered, and touched a button on the goggles. The thumb drive flashed and began to emit small noises. "It's working," he said.

James consulted his cell phone. He scratched his armpits. "Yah. The program's uploading to the goggles."

"How long?" asked Timothie, munching on the other half of the sandwich. He poured half a glass of chilled Chardonnay wine and gulped it. Maude stared.

"About fifteen minutes," said Carmen. "We did it, guys."

James grinned. "Yeah, it's a big program. One of the largest I've ever worked on. Took us a couple of all-nighters to perfect it before we came over here, and then we ran into the passwords and the firewalls. Almost unbreakable. But hey, we're a genius."

"At least I hope it's perfect." Liam brushed back his unruly ginger hair with a freckled hand. "A lot depends on us, hey, Maude? Timothie?"

"You better believe it, dear."

"Yah," Timothie agreed. "I couldn't have done it alone." He adjusted the Cloak of Power. His rose tattoo gleamed on the bulging biceps that strained at his navy polka dot tee-shirt. Maude wore a purple pantsuit and was barefoot on the tiled floors. She fidgeted.

"No more lone rangers," she agreed. Carmen grinned. Her two friends gathered around their tablets and iPhones, excitedly counting down the minutes as the bar eased upward on the green graph that slashed the screens in half.

Timothie frowned. "Do you think this will really delete Reginald's program?"

"It will. And replace it with something much better."

"Liam, your granny loves you," Maude declared. She placed a withered hand on her friend's grandson's shoulder. "I told Timothie you could do it."

"With some help," acknowledged Liam, indicating his two companions. James and Carmen smiled broadly. They punched one another on the back.

Ding

"It's done!" exclaimed James.

The bar flashed into place on the graph and settled, blinking, and the goggles emitted a high-pitched squeal.

Timothie frowned. "What's that?"

"Just the program asserting itself," said Carmen. "I'm satisfied. What about you, dudes?"

"Let's try it out," ventured James. He passed the goggles to Liam, who took them in his shaking hands and placed them over his green eyes. Silence ensued for long minutes.

"I'll be darned," muttered Liam. He began to improvise a dance. His Nike Sweet Classic Hi sneakers shuffled on the brown tiled floor, and he held the arms of the goggles with both hands as he belted a few lines from "Baby One More Time." Then, realizing his exuberance, he blushed and sat down.

"What now?" Timothie elbowed him aside and grasped the goggles.

"Hey, dude, that's rude."

"Sorry, darling, but this is my game now."

"No, it isn't," James said, laughing, and stood up and hugged Maude, then pounded Timothie on his bulging biceps. "This game belongs to the world now."

"Let's see." Timothie placed the yellow goggles over his dark eyes.

Yes, psychedelic lights flashed, and rainbow tunes played. Not in an obsessive fashion, the lights played out as a stream of consciousness that signaled Peace and Freedom and release from fear. A message pulsed from the controls of anger for the establishment and desire to do the right thing, a desire to do good versus evil, and the goggles pulsed with excitement as an Angel of God appeared in front of Timothie's eyes and smiled benignly on *the world.*

Let go, the message beamed to the world at large through the master goggles, which had been activated by the secret switch at the back of the controls, and by the Master Program that washed over them in beta waves with binaural beats for alertness.

Suddenly, the world was alerted to the danger that stalked them in the form of a man demon in a far country called Eparitrea, where a President obsessed with power and megalomania overshadowed the United States and the lesser Dennis Ducksworth, the lesser Justin Harper of Canada, and the lesser U.K. Prime Minister Thelma Louise. A small African country threatened Uriel and the throne of God, as Bael in demonic lust consumed its resources and intelligence, its military force, and its transcendental power from forces long buried in the human condition where humanity began approximately six million years ago.

It wasn't the threat of American nuclear retaliation that measured the pace of the demon Bael, but the threat of a small unknown country that could be likened to that of the birthplace of Jesus Christ of Nazareth. Can any good come out of Nazareth, and can any evil come out of the cradle of hominoids, in an emerging African country that even now threatened the peace of nations with its secrets of nuclear power?

Canada had sent the uranium to Eparitrea for the peaceful use of reactors designed to power generators, lights, and factories, and the CIA had sent weapons of mass destruction to bring about democracy in the small country, under the thumb of Abimbola Patrick, now demagogue.

Timothie mused as he allowed the soothing tones of the new program to course through his skull. "So, Bael used his subtle powers to surprise the nations of Earth with a tiny emerging superpower that would be supremely grateful for the evil devices he supplied."

"That's what the goggles seem to say, dude," agreed Liam, brushing a lock of hair from his eyes.

"But, hey, bro, isn't it *awful* hot in here?"

Flames sizzled in a corner, and Bael's black oozing presence signaled they were not alone. Waves of heat overcame the five people, and they drooped in their chairs like ragdoll cats, not as beautiful, but seemingly as boneless, until, dripping in sweat, Maude raised a helpless hand.

"Stop," she said.

"Stop?" asked Timothie and laughed. His eyes were maniacal.

"Oh, for gosh sake, Tim, get a hold of yourself," Maude commanded.

"It's too much, sweetheart," he groaned, and his cloak flapped in wild circles, settling in a black and gilded cloud onto the floor. Bael roared to life and enveloped the room.

Give me back my power, he bellowed. *The spells, they are mine.*

"No," Maude was adamant. "No, they are not." She stood with her breasts thrust outward and her back straight. "The spells are broken. They were broken by humans, good humans, and good will always overcome evil."

Bael groaned.

"We don't need Uriel," Timothie realized, his brow pale and the sweat streaming in rivulets between his shoulder blades. "He's left the good in us to overcome anything that Bael might send. I felt evil for a moment there, and it was exhilarating. I can sympathize with Reginald. But the God force in me denied it."

"The source of Bael's strength is broken, not by angels but by humanity, who stand for God and all the archangels and angels in Heaven, the charms of the saints that cannot be broken, that have existed since time began, since we worshipped God in the form of trees, winds, and stars."

Correct, moaned Bael and oozed across the floor.

Timothie stamped on the black, putrid liquid full of white and red eyes. The mess came up over his boots and then sloshed back again, making its way to the corner that pulsed with heat. He realized his cloak was still on the tiled floor, underneath the boiling black mass, and his cloak negated the evil that crawled over it until Bael had no choice but to retreat.

The superhero rescued his garment and shook it over the room, scattering bits of dead meat and putrid pus through the steaming air. The cloak whipped and snapped into place, clean and satiny once more. Timothie stowed it in his gym bag, then changed his mind and threw the clean cape over his shoulders.

His cloak cleaned itself, he thought, and all the powers of Hell couldn't dirty it for long. It was a force for good. All this time, he wore the Millennial Goggles; the new and so gentle program coursed through his brain, soothed him and gave him the power of God Almighty.

"You never threatened His throne," he accused, and the puddle of steaming tar in the corner wrinkled and disappeared. "Five is the magic number. Five of blundering and fallible humanity have got together and defeated you, mighty demon. Tremble in Hell. They say there are five types of people now living in America. Five to damn you back to Hell. The Elites, the Consumers, the fear-filled Mass, the criminals and terrorists, and the lone wolves – those individuals who think for themselves and are the most dangerous to the Establishment of all. '*Full fathom five thy father lies; Of his bones are coral made; Those are pearls that were his eyes; Nothing of him that does fade, But doth suffer a sea-change Into something rich and strange.*' "

The corner was curiously clear. The goggles hummed. The box of goggles on the corner of the table had come to life, flashing blue lights and dinging. The program coursed through the Wi-Fi in the room and out through the ether into the eyes and ears of six billion people, who awoke as one to a new understanding and a new certainty.

"What happened?" asked Maude, rubbing her violet-blue eyes. She pulled her left earlobe, tapped her foot, and frowned.

"I think we just won the first battle," Timothie said. He sat, his cloak swirling about him. The gold cross on the back glimmered and glittered. The silver stars glowed. The black background settled into a neutral cloud of power.

"Good," Maude said. "Hungry, Carmen? Thirsty?"

"I think I'll settle in for a good cold Dr. Pepper," Carmen said. "And one of your delicious roast beef and cheese sandwiches, Mrs. Maude."

"Yeah, the temperature musta dropped twenty degrees already," agreed James. "Hey, man, Timothie, you want to take a look at this?"

"I would, darling," Timothie said, "but I seem to have a bit of fatigue right now. Don't want to look at the tablet. Don't want to look at your cell or at my Android. Just want to relax here in my Cloak of Power and decide what we'll do next."

"No, really," James said. "It's cool."

"My gosh, it's a rainbow unicorn on the screen," exclaimed Carmen. "How'd you do that? Two minutes ago, we were looking at the Millennial Goggles from the inside."

"This *is* the Millennial Goggles from the inside," insisted James. Liam looked over his shoulder and agreed.

"What happened to the game?"

"It's a new game, man," said Liam, pointing a finger to the screen. "A rainbow unicorn bringing us peace instead of nuclear weapons."

"A rainbow unicorn? That's for kids or old hippies."

"No, really. It's a symbol of a new age."

"Oh, really?" asked Timothie and wiped a weary hand over his forehead. "It's at least twenty degrees cooler in here. I think I'll open a window, though. Let in some fresh air."

"Let in the rainbow unicorn," Maude said and grinned crookedly. Her old hands expertly massaged Timothie's neck.

"That feels good," he said. The window snicked open as Liam rose and let in the fresh night air, fragrant with the breath of blossoms from below and wafting from the river valley across the ravine.

Maude poured two glasses of white full-bodied Chardonnay wine.

"Let's celebrate."

"Sure," Timothie agreed, and raised his glass.

Chapter Twenty-Nine

Timothie's old nemesis, Reginald Smith, wasn't done yet. He was not too much of a bright fellow, but sly, played both sides of the wall and sat on the wall, indeed, as would the legendary Mugwump.

The holy water swirled in a basin on the other side of his grandiose living room, ready for Bael's appearance at any time. The goggles, useless now, lay on a yellow hassock by the blue and white striped sofa, consumed in small envelopes of flame that flickered but never burned.

Reginald perched in the white velvet recliner, hands on both sides of his face. His forehead wrinkled as he squinted at the blue and white tiles in the center of the room, shining and pristine, sloped to a drain in the middle of the floor, and now bubbling with sodden ash.

"The friggin' goggles sing of peace," complained Reginald. "The skies are rainbow colored now when I look through them, and the fear and anger we felt is gone. The game leads to a conclusion and satisfaction, and over all the world people are throwing off their goggles and staring reality in the face rather than la la land, which is why they were developed. Our synapses no longer connect to the Eparitrean vibes from a country deep in Africa, where we thought we'd be undetected. The six billion souls I promised Bael are lost now to the cause. Someone has cracked an uncrackable code. Neuromarketing and neuroscience be damned, I can't connect the electrodes to the proper brainwaves anymore. Something has interrupted them. Not only interrupted but rerouted the whole routine to another program. Suddenly people are waking up. The far left is no longer inciting the far right, and the far right is no longer racist and violent."

He groaned.

The ashes moved. "It's a perfect photo op moment."

"What do you mean?" Reginald turned to his laptop, blue screen sparkling with emojis and patterns. He flipped open his iPhone and took a selfie. "Satisfied now, big ugly demon?"

"No, look at your screen. The Canadian Broadcasting Corporation," urged the ashes.

The morning CBC news with Petra Womansbridge. Justin Harper climbing a rock wall, his handsome visage pressed to the face of the cliff, wearing yellow goggles, and *smiling*.

"Smiling into the cliff. So what? The women think he's hot."

"Look closer."

He was wearing a fanny pack with *Republic of Eparitrea* emblazoned in gold on the soft black leather, and the official seal of President Abimbola Patrick peeked out from under the gold clasp.

"I'll be darned."

Reginald stood up. His bare toes dug into the soft white, yellow, and blue Scandinavian rug in front of the sofa. Petra's voice chattered from the speakers, and then a commercial began for a pink foamy liquid that would clean out your pipes promptly and with no funny aftertaste.

"Awkward."

After hitting the power button with some force, Reginald slammed the laptop shut and sent it skittering across the bare tiles, into the pile of sodden ash where it was consumed.

Bael burped and regurgitated the computer.

"I think I should lose weight," Bael observed.

Reginald reached for the slimy computer. "You eat too much."

"Do you see what I mean, human? Your leaders are connected to the forces in Africa, to that minuscule country where you chose to hide the nature of our agreement. Now what do you do, flaky little man? Your leader is wearing the yellow goggles, making photo ops and selfies well into the week that was destined for destruction. I wonder what they show him."

"We know that." Reginald wiped at the mucous covering his laptop and stared at the image of the man in power in Canada. "They're showing him peace and reality and goodness. They've demolished the darn program."

The ashes turned to ebony and began to swirl across the room. "His arrogance maybe covers up the changes in the program. There still might be a chance. Why else would he so extravagantly wear the symbol of mankind's arch enemy?"

"He might be trying to send us a message."

"Indeed. There'll be a dreadful war in Heaven if we succeed. Billions of souls will scream and fall in agony, or triumph and wear the crowns of perdition. I promised you eternal life and money beyond the furthest stretches of your imagination if you hand me the six billion souls, Mr. Smith, but it looks as though Timothie Hill and his friends have dashed that hope. With the little expectancy we have left, I want you to find the connection between the Prime Minister and the Republic of Eparitrea. I want you to see if this disaster that befell us last night could be reversed."

"You're the almighty demon. Why can't you do it?"

The ebony slime continued to bubble. The remainder of the ashes swirled down the drain. Reginald's hand reached for the basin of holy water in the corner of the room.

"Don't."

"I'm damned anyway, aren't I?" Reginald threw the whole basin of holy water onto the simmering black mess. Bael screamed and was silent. The shining blue and white tiles showed no evidence of the grossness that had occupied the center only a moment before.

"No, you're not," a soft voice murmured, and Reginald looked up with wild red eyes to see a silken Angel hovering over the room. He ran to a corner cabinet, and inserted a large key into the hole. Inside there was a Colt Diamondback .38 Special revolver, the ammunition stored in a case underneath. He inserted the bullets, grasped the .38 in both hands, and held it to his left temple.

"That's not a good idea, my dear young man." Uriel beamed at him.

"You're too kind," Reginald gasped. "I'm doomed."

He pulled the trigger.

Time is relative, certainly to God and his angels. Einstein knew that decades ago, and Planck and Heisenberg certainly made a dent in our knowledge of how time is not like a river nor is it like an arrow, but circular and sometimes we see the backs of our own heads if we look far enough ahead. Reginald gazed into the barrel of the Diamondback .38 Special and saw only hopelessness and release, but Uriel saw a circle of time in a puff of smoke. She put out a huge soft hand and stopped the bullet before it spun from the damaged bore. The rest of the gun blew up in Reginald's hand. He dropped the fragments and lay, stunned, his head on a cushion that had fallen off the sofa.

"Why am I still alive? The damn gun exploded in my hand."

"Everyone has a second chance. If not in Heaven, then on Earth."

"You saved me. But you put me to a task I can't accomplish."

Uriel put her arms around the prostrate man. "Get up, Reginald. You have work to do."

"Yeah, Bael wants me to scope out Justin Harper. Find the connection to President Patrick of Eparitrea. That's a diplomatic mission I'm not equipped to do. He wants me to be a spy and star in a thriller movie."

"You've already done enough for the demon. Be a man. You can make amends."

"How? I've double-crossed my old friend Timothie and his pals, I've betrayed my country and mankind, I've made a pact with the Devil, and I tried to overthrow Heaven. How can I make amends?" Reginald staggered to his feet within the safety of Uriel's arms.

"You were deceived," murmured the soft low voice into his ear. "Without you, Liam and his friends would never have been able to program the goggles to overthrow the prime agenda that had been broadcast to all humanity, even to those who were immune."

"But our leaders, they're still..."

"Appearances can deceive as well. You don't know, either, what President Ducksworth has done with this new knowledge. It's a knowledge that is now broadcast to all the world, to all leaders, all countries, including our main connection, Eparitrea. Why would your Prime Minister climb a rock face wearing a device that has your enemy's seal on it– to show all the world, perhaps, the real danger when he's been temporarily silenced by politics?"

"Yes, I hadn't thought of that."

"Even now, there's a coup going on in Eparitrea."

"Let me see." Reginald opened his laptop, and the screen flashed to the CBC news. Pictures of pink laughing bunnies bounced across the monitor. "I'm impatient."

"Of course. You are man."

"Here it is. Breaking news."

Petra Womansbridge's earnest face relaxed into a smile. "...has just announced at the White House that all barricades to immigration have been relaxed for the second half of his tenure. His generals have responded to the negotiations for nuclear disarmament with the Russians and the North Koreans by eradicating all barriers to transparency. The Chinese have extended a further three trillion dollars as collateral for the United State's massive debt, and the interest has been forgiven.

"In news closer to home, Prime Minister Harper has spoken in Vancouver for the second time on the importance of interracial harmony and has declared Nazism illegal in Canada, with severe penalties for civil disobedience. This appears to be a step in the right direction, according to Professor Emeritus Russell Bertram of the University of Laval, Quebec. Our former tolerance of any and all diversity appears to be conforming to a more realistic approach of security and safety for homegrown Canadians and naturalized citizens who are peaceful at heart and don't desire hatred or fear to rule – or ruin – their beloved country."

"What have we done?" Reginald gasped and began to pick at the pieces of the revolver that had exploded in his hands. He wiped the soot from his face. "It worked!"

His hands were covered in black soot. "Why isn't my face burned?" he asked. Uriel patted his shoulder.

"See my hands."

Reginald gasped. The Angel's hands were burned and twisted.

"You took the bullet for me!"

"Will you heal?" Reginald continued. "You will, won't you?"

The Angel smiled like the Mona Lisa, inexplicable, not gloating, but on the verge. "In time we all heal."

"What does that mean?"

"Heaven only knows, Mr. Smith." And she disappeared.

Chapter Thirty

Paula and Skye bustled about their little rooms in the back of Timothie's hair salon and spa as they prepared for the busy day ahead. A key clicked in the rear door, and their boss appeared.

"What's this?" He plugged in the kettle and scooped ground Espresso coffee into the stainless-steel French press. "All ready for the day without being asked?"

"Aren't we always?" Skye posed in her new pink scrubs, hair to match, a fancy headband across her wide forehead.

"Yes," Paula agreed, putting out the tools of her pedicure trade. "It's a lovely day to be at work, Tim. Did you hear the news? Our Prime Minister, Mr. Harper, has warned us against Eparitrea and said that he couldn't say anything until a photo op yesterday. He said he wore the badge of the enemy so we would remember that the uranium we sold to President Patrick last year was a mistake, and that all is now well, but he couldn't mention the name of the country until now. He said that the world situation has turned on a flashpoint, and what was wrong is now right. He also said he was taking his family to New York for a vacation and he's meeting Dennis Ducksworth there to play miniature golf with their children. A great photo op, I think, for all of them."

Timothie arched one manicured eyebrow and hitched at his camouflage pants with the Converse stars in the pockets. "Love not hate," he murmured as he poured the bubbling liquid into the glass container.

"That's what your shirt says and that's what we say," Paula continued. He glanced about the clean and sparkling white room. No goggles in sight.

"What happened last night? Where are they all?"

"Oh, you mean these?" Paula opened a drawer and took out a pair of the yellow-rimmed glasses. "We don't need them anymore. They're no fun anyhow. We figured out we'd been duped."

"Duped?"

"Yes. We sort of woke up yesterday morning, as soon as we got to work and tried to play the game. It didn't play anymore, and we didn't feel that woozy emotion that made us all giddy and ready to please anybody who told us what to do."

Skye interrupted. "We don't need anybody to tell us what to do."

Timothie was curious. "How did it feel?"

"Like waking up from a bad dream." Skye swished a clean cloth over the countertop. "The game wasn't fun anymore, that took my mind off what I was doing and focused on – well – obedience. That sucked me down a deep, dark rabbit hole into another world. Where I didn't know my own mind."

"What happened?"

"I don't know. All of a sudden, the game didn't work anymore. I just saw rainbows and prisms through the glasses and heard the sound of my own breathing. My brain kind of hummed a peaceful song, and then everything was quiet, and I knew that the spell was broken."

"It was awful," agreed Paula. "It was worse than smoking or drinking. It was a drive that clouded all my judgment. In the back of every emotion I felt there was fear. Fear that I wouldn't be good enough, fear that I would offend somebody higher up, fear that I wouldn't get the game right and we would all die."

Timothie sipped at a cup of black coffee, fresh from the stainless-steel Bodum with the sturdy glass canister. "Why did you keep wearing them then, if they made you feel that bad?"

"I couldn't stop. And it wasn't all bad, Tim. Why, the feeling that you get when you first put the goggles on is a rush like your first heroin shot must be like, a rush like I've never felt before. Then you're drawn into the rushing pyramids and angles of the game, the colors and crazy shapes and sounds."

"Sounds?"

"Yes, there was sounds, too. Like nothing else heard outside of an Angel band. I could see through the goggles to the world outside, but it didn't matter so much anymore. Nothing mattered except getting the angles right, the colors aligned, the sounds in the right order, and the click in my brain when it all went well. Then the feeling of peace and surrender."

"Surrender to what?" Timothie scratched his chest. He knew but had never understood the lure of the goggles.

"Why, Timothie. I don't really know. There was always something important. More important than us. More important than you and my work and my family and friends. It lured me down that rabbit hole but never satisfied. Sometimes I would feel angry, for no reason, and then someone would come into the room, or something would pop up on the internet, and I'd know why I was angry. It didn't make much sense afterward. But at the time, I would focus all my rage on whatever the glasses told me was wrong."

"Like what?"

She hung her head. "Other races, mostly. Like Mr. and Mrs. Cardinal, your clients in the other room. They're native Canadian, aren't they? For no reason, I hated them. Wanted to hurt them."

"I didn't know that." Timothie frowned. Paula threw the goggles into the wastebasket. They boomed like a gong as they ricocheted against the far side.

"Or your friend Dareboy."

"Jack?"

"Yes, Crazy Jack. He's a black man, so handsome, so lithe, so muscular. But so different from what the goggles told us was right."

"They taught hatred?"

"Hatred and fear. I don't know which was stronger."

Timothie pursed his lips and frowned again. "That's sickening."

"I know. I woke up yesterday morning, put the goggles on, and a rush of love came over me. I knew then that what I had felt was just a bad dream, the goggles were telling me it wasn't right to hate or fear, and they sang a song of such peace. A peace that I had been looking for without success for many weeks as I wore them."

"They promised you peace?"

Skye interrupted as she gnawed on a broken pink nail. "Yes, that's all they promised, peace from the hatred and fear if we followed their game to the end. But there was never an end, and we were just like robots finally, waiting for a sign, waiting for someone to come and punch our buttons and we would act. Without thought."

"Act without thought." Timothie mused then hitched up the camo pants over his white leather shoes. His white tee-shirt with the "Love Not Hate" slogan in red seemed appropriate now, in light of what his two assistants were telling him.

A bell sounded, a small *ding* in the ensuing silence. "I think that's the Cardinals now," he said. "They're at the front door, right on time. Mrs. Cardinal wants a manicure and a pedi, and George just wants to chat. He's bald as the hills in Saskatchewan, will never be a hair client."

Paula smiled. "Send her in. She has beautiful long hair. Maybe she'll sit in your chair out front when we're finished here, have the grey touched up."

"Yes." He strode past the surrealistic paintings on the wall of the lobby, past the mirror, past the chestnut vines to the front, and opened the glass doors. "Welcome!"

Mr. and Mrs. Cardinal held hands. Curious again, as always, Timothie asked, "How long have you two been married?"

Shy now, George and Clara glanced at one another with eyes as brown and liquid as pools under starlight. George squeezed his wife's shoulder. "It'll be fifty years in October."

"Amazing. You're still so much in love."

"Don't know how I've put up with him all these years," declared Mrs. Cardinal.

"She must be crazy," George agreed and laughed. "Now go on and get your toenails done, sweetheart. I'll just sit down in this here chair and talk to Timothie."

"I envy you," Timothie admitted. "I've never been married."

"Oh, it's the best thing ever happened to me. I remember, as a young pup I was pretty wild. You know those glasses you sold me?"

"I sold them to you?"

"Well, yes, in a manner of speaking. One of your girls in the back there got out a box of them and sold me two pair for ten dollars. Worst money I ever spent. The whole time I wore them I thought of nothing but my younger days, when I was a wild 'un. Full of guilt and remorse, I was, and then just plain old-fashioned anger and fear. Nothing good ever comes of that. I was harsh with my wife, harsh with our children, harsh with myself. Just waiting to be told what to do and following that cursed game down the rabbit hole.

"Rabbit hole? Someone else called it that."

"That's what you thought of when you wore them. Like Alice in Wonderland."

Timothie plopped down in the silver chair opposite Mr. Cardinal. "Interesting."

"Then it all changed. Yesterday morning, it was. We got up, as usual, me earlier than Clara, and I made us tea as usual. She grumped about in her housecoat for a while then, as usual, we slipped on those yellow-rimmed goggles with the red lenses. And lo and behold. Nothing happened out of the ordinary. Not really. But angels sung, I could have sworn, and the colors all went like a rainbow and prisms, and something just brought us a huge feeling of peace like we'd never known for the two months we wore those cursed things. They always promised us peace, but we never found it, though we waited and tried to come to the end of the game, where we thought it was."

"What? Peace?"

"Well, yes. The promise was always there; if we did things right, we'd be rewarded. I know addictions. My brother was an alcoholic for thirty years until he went on the program. This was just like that, only worse. We couldn't put them down for more than fifteen minutes at a time without feeling this awful sense of doomsday. The only relief was when we put them on. We could see through them, of course, do our work and daily chores. But mostly we just wanted to veg. You know."

"Vegetate?"

"Yeah. It was like we were waiting for something that was going to happen any minute. Someone was going to tell us what to do. There'd be nuclear war if we didn't do it right. They used fear and hatred to control us. The colored angles and shapes, the pyramids swirled in our brains, and the numbers crunched too quick for us to read them, the urgency of it, then the long waiting for another round of instructions."

George Cardinal crossed his long legs. His socks were white, and Timothie saw a hole in one of the heels that showed under the strap of his sandals.

"See that?" he asked. "Hole in my socks. We let everything go. Didn't care about a thing. The whole world sort of ground to a halt, didn't it? Lazy, lackadaisical people trying to work, trying to make the world go 'round, and just like that, everything stalled when the yellow goggles came on the market. I don't know where they came from or who first discovered them. I don't remember them being advertised, they were just there all of a sudden, and everyone had to have a pair."

"It was word of mouth," Timothie said. "But I've seen ads, too. Big ads on billboards, ads on the internet, ads on TV."

"Yeah? Maybe you're right. I forget."

"Everyone forgets. It's not just you, Mr. Cardinal."

"George." He scratched his head, which gleamed like a crystal ball. Timothie screwed up his face and frowned.

"George. Very interesting. Thanks for letting me know all this. I wasn't affected, you see. A small minority of us weren't."

"Lucky you."

Timothie nodded. "It started a few months ago. And it ended yesterday. Suddenly."

"Yes, that's about right. Yesterday morning. I noticed my mailman, too, he came up the walk whistling like he used to, and not wearing those damn glasses."

"It must have been like a nightmare."

"Oh, it was," George said. "Except we never woke up from it. Until yesterday."

Mrs. Cardinal was at the door leading from the spa. Her nails shone and her face glowed. "Here's my sweetie," she chirped. She pirouetted in front of the two men. "What do you think?"

"Nice nails," George opined. "I like the color."

She wore flimsy spa slippers to allow her toenails to dry. They were the same salmon pink as her fingernails. She wore a salmon pink patterned dress. Her lips were scarlet and her eyes sparkled. "You're beautiful, darling," Timothie cried.

George smiled. "I'm a lucky man."

"I have an idea." Timothie broke open a can of diet Pepsi and sipped. "Why don't you two come back to the salon later today? You know the group of us that got together at my place a couple of weeks ago? With Maude McKenna and Hilda's grandson and his friends? And the rest of her great pals from the lodge and her bridge club? You know Maude."

"Why, yes, we know Maude McKenna. But what's that got to do with us? I know Hilda's grandson, Carmen, too, and the other boys he chums with. But we don't know anything about a group that got together at your place. We must have been left out." Mrs. Cardinal took George's hand and played with the cufflinks on his shirt. "I don't know what you mean, Timothie. But we'll be glad to come back to the salon this afternoon. I thought I might get my hair color touched up. Paula suggested it and it's a good idea. I've neglected my appearance for the past couple of months."

"We all have," George agreed. "But what's up?"

"Just an idea I have," Timothie said. "I thought I'd get another group together."

"What? Here?"

"No room for all of us," the hair stylist mused. "But there's a place in the river valley I have in mind. A clearing near the golf course. Where the trees all talk to each other."

"Now you're getting weird." George chuckled. "Just like at the Grand Canyon last spring."

Timothie snorted, finished his drink, and crushed the can of Pepsi. "Yes, that was weird. Anything with Crazy Jack Dareboy is weird. But he's come around, last time I saw him, and it's time he got back here from Spain and helped us out again."

"He's a fine boy," Mrs. Cardinal beamed. "He'll help us for sure. With what, Timothie?"

"Oh, I have to think on it for a while, darling. But he'll fly like the wind when I call him. He'll be here fast."

"I know if Jack is here, it'll be all right." George Cardinal shifted in his seat and pulled Clara to his lap. They both got up, he with legs stiff from sitting overlong.

"We can meet here, then go to the river valley where the event will take place tonight."

"What event is that, dear?" Mrs. Cardinal asked.

"Why," said Timothie, "we'll end this game."

"The demon, I think he's talking about." George leaned against the front door, arm around his wife. He shifted from one foot to the other and frowned. "I almost forgot about the demon."

"You know, in all the excitement and everything, so did I, dear." Mrs. Cardinal smoothed her glossy hair behind her ears. "How could we forget the demon that almost emptied the Colorado River in the Grand Canyon, where it feeds into Phoenix and parts of California. Could have been a disaster. Seems to me Crazy Jack was behind that, though, not any demon."

"Believe me, it was a demon behind everything."

"I don't believe in demons, dearie," said Mrs. Cardinal.
"Did you see the river boil?"
She shuddered and whispered, "We'll be back here tonight."

Chapter Thirty-One

Reginald whispered in a corner of his penthouse, near the basin now empty of holy water. He knew a priest at the Basilica who supplied him with blessings for his stock of the precious liquid, knowing little of the demon he supported, but guessing the urgency of the request. On few occasions had Reginald felt the need or the desire to dump the entire contents on the flaccid form of Bael, but a few hours ago he had done so. The remnants of the sodden ashes had long ago washed down the drain. But Reginald still held in his mind the horrible stench and dreadful noises the demon uttered before dissolving into particles of trash that flushed down to Hell.

"What have I done?" The fair-haired man whimpered. He followed with his eyes the recent ascension of the white-winged Angel, Uriel, so lately present in holy compassion.

He peered into a small mirror that lay on a corner table. Soot still remained on Reginald's cheek. He rubbed it off onto a peach-colored towel that he kept near the basin and mirror. He would make amends.

The home page of his iPhone offered him a few choices of contacts, one of which was his old friend Timothie Hill. He wasn't sure Timothie would welcome a call from him, but he had nowhere else to turn. His boss at TopStrategy Marketing had been supplanted by Reginald himself, and he had not endeared himself to the top management nor the middle managers of the company, nor, indeed, the staff who kept the wheels of the enterprise truly turning.

His only noteworthy accomplishment in the world of marketing had been the Millennial Goggles, and those now, thanks in great part to his mismanagement, were defunct in the world to which they had been dedicated as pariah to God himself. Yes, it was mismanagement, or perhaps guilt, that had coerced Reginald into helping with Liam's data, resulting in a program that effectively took down the entire scheme.

Reginald shook his head. He was on the wall again, driven both ways, totally indecisive without the guiding hand of his demon to stabilize him. He knew how valuable he had become to the dark side. A trick of fate had led him from the Ouija board as a teen to tarot cards and incantations under a full moon as a young man, then to darker and deeper secrets discovered in a coven of women who had long since quit his experiments in horror.

Reginald's mother – brooding, pale, and gifted – had bequeathed him this strange power. Only after he had accidentally come upon an ancient book of Satanic spells in a cupboard in her boudoir had Reginald known the strange excitement and horror of courting genuine evil. Still, his mother, long dead now, had bequeathed him something more – a keen curiosity and an equally keen conscience, not compatible with his recent wickedness.

Written in his mother's spidery handwriting, he had discovered a slip of paper with the spell to conjure Bael, a demon of gigantic proportions and well imbued with legend, being present in the Christian Bible as well as ancient manuscripts from the middle East. That Bael would grant him invisibility then take it away he knew very well. That Bael would haunt his waking moments and drive all restful sleep and peaceful dreams from his tortured and hot brain he also knew all too well. The black, liquid, putrid form that the demon often took repulsed Reginald, and he saw in the many white and red eyespots the means by which he could never escape surveillance into his soul. His wretched soul, for Reginald, until last night, had been convinced that all hope for salvation was now beyond him.

Now he wasn't so sure that Heaven escaped his immortal grasp. Uriel had been so kind and so comforting. She had said that everyone could be healed. Reginald jerked his head to glance once around the room, but it was empty. Empty of both good and evil.

Good.

The goggles were useless now, and the six billion souls he had promised to Bael were lost. In part because of him, and Bael knew that. The demon's response would be swift and merciless when it no longer needed the man. His one hope was to hang onto a shred of usefulness to the dark side.

He shook his head.

Bael must believe that all was not lost, that the war would be won, the Armageddon he envisioned for the almighty throne of the universe and all universes beyond this, could still be secured. Reginald's mouth twitched, his stomach heaved, and he grasped the basin and vomited into the shiny bowl. With shaking hands, he wiped his mouth and mustache with the towel.

He didn't feel any better.

Uriel, the man whispered, hardly daring to hope he would be heard. Thunder crashed in the distance and mighty wings boomed.

My son.

"How can you love me after what I've done? After what I've become? I'm a worm in your sight, mighty Angel. I have missed the mark. I have erred. I have sinned."

Your confession is from a clean heart, Reginald Smith. Your repentance is all we require. You're healed. Now clean yourself, then come with me.

Was it really that simple? Reginald lifted his head, hardly daring to believe, but the Angel smiled at him and poured from her great sleeve a basin of warm clean water, washed Reginald's face and hands tenderly, then dried him with the hem of her robe. The man rose to his feet. His face shone with a new, steady light.

"What do I do?" he asked.

Uriel wrapped him in an embrace and whispered in his ear, "You're an old soul, Mr. Smith, but your redemption is young. Give yourself time to feed from the milk of faith and truth. Then like an arrow from a bow, fly straight and true to the heart of evil, smash it into a thousand shards like a sun exploding into a supernova, into a dark hole, destroy the evil, Reginald, with your blinding light. Only you can undo the wrong, because only you created it."

"No, it's too difficult," Reginald complained and pushed the Angel away. "I can't do it. I'm afraid."

"We are all afraid. Even the archangels are afraid when Hell rumbles under Earth. Take hold of your fear and pour it out like water through sand, my dear."

"Why can't you do it?"

"There's something beyond Heaven that holds us in its rule. We cannot cross the barrier between Angel and demon. Only a human can do that. Only you, Reginald."

"I'm too weak. I'll never do it. I'll never be able to stand up to Bael and all his other demons that he controls. Timothie can do it."

The Angel smiled. "Timothie is strong and has the Cloak of Power. But it will not serve him to overcome the dark force that has been unleashed through your manipulations. Only your friendship with Timothie and your love will do that. Now go and conquer, man."

"No. I cannot."

But Uriel was gone, and Reginald stood alone at the large window overlooking the district of Oliver in downtown Edmonton, the traffic below crawling like fleas on a dog's hindquarters. Jasper Avenue snaked to the north and around to Stony Plain Road where finally Reginald lost sight of the blank-faced buildings. He sighed and trembled and glanced repeatedly at the pentagram in the middle of the blue and white tiled floor, the symbol of demonic power he had constructed soon after buying the condo.

With shaking hands, he dialed Timothie's number, half hoping that his former friend would not answer, half praying that he would and rescue him. His astrological sign also was embedded next to the pentagram, the sign of Pisces, the most spiritual sign in the Zodiac. He was born on March 16, under a moon in Pisces, a wounded idealist, sensitive and selfish, rather silly in his humor, which he kept in check at all times consistent with the demands of his twelfth house. *Indeed, many would say I have no sense of humor as puns and slapstick are not thought by some to be funny.* Then he grinned and made a loud farting noise into the phone as Timothie answered.

Chapter Thirty-Two

As a last-minute gathering of friends of Timothie and Dareboy, the group was a success. They came together in the funky salon, sat wherever they could grab a seat, some by the geraniums, some by the horse chestnut vines, and some on the actual chairs that Timothie supplied.

Julie Ann Carter, with her bad back, reclined painfully in the armchair and admired her dainty feet as she stretched them in front of her. With kisses and plentiful hugs, she was prone to call her acquaintances and friends of both genders, "honey." She balanced a large glass of iced tea on her lap with a plate of scones. She passed the scones occasionally to Maude's next-door neighbor in the lodge, Heather Ellen Armstrong.

Heather Ellen sported salt and pepper hair, looked younger than her age, but walked with a cane, stooped over from degenerated discs in her back and osteoporosis. She sang in the seniors' chorus, the Darling Clementines, with their other neighbor, Ben O'Hara. Heather had a soft speaking voice, difficult to hear, but could belt out an old-time gospel song as though the building had no roof.

Ben – pudgy, average height, good sense of humor but a real curmudgeon, retired as a clinical psychologist 10 years ago, liked good Scotch and good food, and wore black rubber clogs for comfort. He had hip problems and used a walker.

There was the German woman, Hilda Hermann, as well as the dignified Ross Murray and his doting wife Jenny. Ross and Jenny had been called from dinner at their home by the highway. Santiago Florian and his wife Patricia Florian also were called from their retirement condo at Horizon Village on the southside, where they had been entertaining seniors with their guitar, banjo, and hilarious old songs. They brought along a young friend, Christian Colombo, who sang and played a classic guitar. The group was rounded off by Maude and her ash blonde hair, now with streaks of royal blue, and Hilda's grandson, Liam, and his two pals, Carmen and James.

"So, everyone's here," announced Timothie with satisfaction. He looked around. Hmmm. No Mr. and Mrs. Cardinal. No Dareboy. Reginald was on his way – he had just called from the penthouse in downtown Oliver district, and Timothie knew Reginald could *fly* with his new yellow Lamborghini. Reginald had called him. Reginald would be here, contrite but full of pizzazz as he was, a real asset to the team Timothie and Maude had put together.

The glass front door rattled and Crazy Jack Dareboy strode in, late as usual, but heaving with satisfaction at the long flight from Barcelona. He, of course, had not flown traditionally, but had transported himself with much aplomb from the villa on the outskirts of the city to Timothie's salon in Edmonton in less than an hour. Dripping with perspiration, Dareboy adjusted his scarlet jumpsuit and grinned.

"I'll have a beer," he announced, and Timothie saw to it that he had a very cold beer in hand before he turned his attention once more to the door. Clara and George Cardinal were arm in arm at the entrance, smiling at the group, rather shy, and Timothie took it upon himself to introduce them to everyone.

There were handshakes all around and more smiles. The Cardinals settled on the bench in front of the large plate glass window, drinks in hand. Reginald arrived. Chatter stopped, and they all looked expectantly at Timothie. He raised his glass in a mock salute.

"Here we are," he began. *What to say?* "You all know why we're here. I've explained as best I could the last time we all got together, and you all saw the damage the demon could do. You don't know the part a friend of mine played in it." He glared at Reginald, who stared back and flushed.

"But that's all over now. We have a big winning hand here. Bael is almost defeated. The Millennial Goggles are a thing of the past now that the world has been set free. The only thing keeping us from complete victory is the power of the dark side that won't admit defeat."

Ross Murray cleared his throat and sneezed. "Hay fever," his wife offered, to no one in particular. "It's all these plants, especially the geraniums."

"It's alright, Mom," Ross said. "Just a tickle in my throat."

"We're going outside to the river valley by the golf course," Timothie said. "Is that going to bother you? I don't want anyone getting sick out there, dear."

"He'll be all right." Patricia Murray sucked on her lower lip. "Here, Daddy, I have your cane."

"Thank you, Jenny."

"He's an old war hero. He didn't have any allergies when we first met. They've crept up on him these last few years we've lived in Sherwood Park. I blame the pesticide spraying and all those chemicals they put on the roads now. What do you think, Ross?"

He chuckled. "You're always right, Mom." Santiago rolled his bright blue eyes.

Maude clapped her hands together. Dareboy jumped and spilled his beer. Carmen, James, and Liam grinned. "Let's go," they said in unison. "We couldn't have done it just the three of us, either, Liam. We needed four, right, Reg?" Liam grinned and ran his ruddy hand through his flaxen hair. The rest of the group straggled through the back door into the alley where they had left their transportation. Some doubled up. Mr. and Mrs. Cardinal drove with Reginald in his Lamborghini, beaming together. She clapped her hands as Maude just had.

"We'll get the truck on the way back," George said. "Can't pass up an opportunity like this one."

"Wow, a Lambo." James passed a hand over his long black hair. Dareboy leaned on the door and grinned. "I'll go with Maude in the Benz," he said. Timothie locked the front door, then was the last out the back, Skye and Paula having long since gone home for the day.

* * *

When they arrived at the clearing in the forest, the group all hunkered down in a circle and looked up at their leader, Timothie, who sat with Reginald on a stump by a grove of birch trees. Reginald held something in his hand that gleamed in the late afternoon light. Ross Murray sneezed. His wife, Jenny, put a protective hand on his arm. "We can't stay long. Dad's not feeling well."

"I'm fine."

"This won't take long." A soft breeze soughed through the silver-green leaves of the birch. They could hear the trickle of water nearby. The golf course and surrounding city were completely hidden by the little forest. "We'll join hands." Timothie planted his leather Converse sneakers on the spongy moss of the clearing. "Follow my lead, darlings."

They all stood, some with canes and walkers, and began to chant. Reginald showed them what was in his hand. Crystals glimmered amongst small silver ingots. Curious crows circled closer, and Ben glanced up at the birds and winced. *The Birds,* he thought. *Alfred Hitchcock. One of my nightmares. Tied to a friggin' bird, an actor without recourse.* He swallowed. Someone snickered and someone else coughed. Then all was silent. From out of the woods drifted small animals, creatures of the late afternoon, a couple of fawns and their mother, a coyote, jackrabbits, and red squirrels.

"Curious," Ben commented.

Maude clutched his hand even tighter. "It is. But don't look at them, Ben. Look at the center of the circle. Look at Reginald and the crystals. They're glowing in his hand."

"Do you see that?" Santiago opened his bright round blue eyes in an expression of mock surprise. "I think he's on fire."

His wife, Patricia Florian, gripped his hand and shook it. "Shush."

The crystals continued to glow. Small animals inched closer. Voices could be heard from the golf course nearby, but nothing could be seen except the grove of birch, the circle of pine and spruce, the straggly limbs of willow and poplar. Wildflowers scattered their colorful petals amongst the dusty green of the fescue – Smooth Fleabane and Gaillordia, buttery dandelions and Meadow Blazingstar. The chanting climbed higher. From the branches of nearby oak rose tiny voices in choruses in reply, so tiny as to be almost indistinguishable from the song of Nuthatch and Purple Finches, which rose in clouds of flurry and feathers from the shrubs and crowns of the trees. The crows circled, black and intelligent.

The grass burned in cinders in the middle of the circle where they danced and sang, voices soaring, joined by fairy voices from all sides. Startled, the young Christian Colombo let go of the hands next to his and stepped from the circle. They all stood indecisively, then stepped back. The two fawns sniffed the warm evening air and their mother followed them past the group of friends to the outer edge of the clearing, then they stood together like three soft tawny statues and stared. Crooning fairies began to slip down the slanted late evening sunbeams to the middle of the grove.

"My god," Maude breathed. "Fairies from Draxxt."

"I don't think so." Timothie motioned them all to be still. The charms sparkled in Reginald's hands. Rainbows arced from the crystals to the tops of the pines. Pine cones clattered to the rocks below.

Suddenly, the shrubs parted. A path opened up. A terrible and dark path, that leaned down from the top of the hill to the depths of an open grave. A huge wild boar crashed through the pines. Its black bristles and red eyes were set forty inches from the ground and it was more than six feet long. It thundered on tiny black cloven feet, great yellow curved tusks on its bottom lip covered with slavering yellow foam as it made for the company of friends. The sound as it came toward them was horrible to hear, grunting and oinking and squealing. Its great head gyrated from side to side and its curly tail sprung straight up from a bony bristled back. Powerful muscles rippled under its horny hide as it charged first Timothie then Reginald.

"You forgot your cloak, Timothie!" screamed Reginald as he tumbled to the ground, the boar on top of him.

"No, I didn't, good friend." The stylist threw his backpack at the boar. The backpack opened up and the silver and gold-spangled cloak dropped out, enveloping both boar and Reginald. "Take this!" He threw himself under the cloak, onto the back of the boar, and rode the beast to the edge of the clearing. It bucked and squealed. The cloak billowed about the pair.

Timothie hollered and hung on. Finally, just as the boar turned to deliver a final crushing blow to its rider, Timothie jumped from its back and hovered high above the trees in midair.

Uncertain, the boar snorted then... *changed.*

Reginald continued chanting, the charms spread on the ground in front of him. To his horror, the boar's cloven feet curved into great claw-like appendages, the boar's dreadful snarling rubbery face melted into putrid black putty, and Bael emerged.

"Why won't you leave me alone?" cried Reginald.

Bael snorted and, in a booming thunder of a voice, replied. It was echoed throughout the glen. The grave that had opened in the earth at the bottom of the emerging path through the woods smoked and burned. It reeked of sulfur. Bael shuddered and the boar reappeared, now more than eighty inches high and nine feet long, weighing what must have been two tons, covered in black bristles, slimy yellow foam, and red piggish eyes that glared like lanterns into the center of the frozen group.

"Heaven only knows, Mr. Smith," the pig grunted and sneered.

Maude screamed. Santiago fainted. Patricia clutched her husband and turned as pale as the cirrus clouds in the sky. Someone began to sing. It was Heather Ellen, soon joined by Ben. *We shall overcome. We shall overcome. We shall overcome. Some day.*

The grove rocked with the Afro American gospel song, and as they sang, the boar slid down the path to the opening of the slope, followed by shining crystals from Reginald's fingers and a spell that snapped and crackled through the glen.

Suddenly, a fairy settled on the back of the monster, dug her little heels into the thick bristly hide, and began to laugh. Her laughter was taken up by the entire glen of tiny creatures. The monster shook its head, scattering spume and foam over the silver gowns of the forest folk. They circled the beast, laughing and singing until the creature could stand no more and slid down the slippery slope into the open grave.

The hole stank with fire and brimstone and opened up into perdition below where the boar sank with a last loud cry. Bael's final earthly body was ridden by fairies and rainbows down, down, until the Earth closed over the hollow it had fallen through and there was only the sound of the nuthatch and warbler left in the grove of birch and pine.

Silence.

"Thank you, Tim." Reginald got to his feet and brushed dirt off his Chinos. His spell hovered like rainbows over the crowns of the small forest trees. The dying strains of "We Shall Overcome" echoed through the clearing. The coyote crept closer. The speckled fawns with their mother turned and bounded into the safety of the shrubs. Snowshoe hare froze in the last rays of the setting sun. The red squirrels chittered amongst the branches of the willows and spruce. A large white moon rose in the east. The golfers were silent. They may have gone home. Maude stretched her arms over her head and called, "Woo hoo!"

"Woo hoo!" They echoed. "We won!"

"No, the fairies carried the day for us," Timothie said, hovering six inches from the speckled fescue and columbine in the groundcover.

"I think they're from your old home planet, Draxxt," Reginald agreed. He pulled on his lower lip.

"I'd recognize them anywhere." Maude smiled, showing straight white natural teeth. "They rode our old nemesis down to Hell. Maybe they redeemed it, who knows?"

"They seemed happy enough about it," agreed Julie Ann. "I think it's our faith that saved us from a fate worse than..."

"Oh, please," Reginald said. "Spare me."

"Sorry. But how else would you explain it? Our rescue was a miracle."

The group murmured agreement amongst themselves, happy to be going home as night descended. Their cars waited in the parking lot by the club house, and they walked, supporting themselves with canes or walkers, and held one another tightly as they made their way back across the little grove to the low brick building with the golf carts parked out front.

"I don't know." Timothie stuffed his cloak into the backpack once more. "I think Uriel might have had something to do with it."

"Like what?" Reginald strode along beside his old friend. He chuckled.

"What's funny?"

"You know my crooked sense of humor. I only know the names of two angels. Hark and Harold."

"Groan."

Reginald laughed. "And Uriel. Say, you know what?"

The yellow Lamborghini purred to life. The Cardinals, uncertain, got into Maude's 1979 Mercedes Benz. The rest of the group somehow scrabbled into various vehicles and they all roared off from the river valley to 97 Avenue then across to Ada Boulevard, because that's where Timothie lived. And Timothie was The Man. Drained to the bone, when they got there, they murmured goodnights, and made their respective ways home.

Timothie plucked his backpack from the Lambo's trunk, while the rest of the crowd dispersed across the city, leaving Reg and him alone to trudge the three flights of stairs up to his apartment.

"What?" Timothie asked his old lover. "I know what?"

"I'm a bit puzzled," said Reginald. "Why didn't Bael kill me when he had the chance?"

"You probably could be useful to him. Still."

"Yeah? You think?"

"Yes. You know, the fairies wouldn't kill him."

They reached the top, and Timothie inserted his key in the lock. It turned smoothly, and they entered the dark room. He switched on the ambient lighting. Reginald smoothed his mustache and adjusted his glasses. "No, I suppose they wouldn't."

"They might rehabilitate him."

"A demon like that? The fairies would do that?"

"Anything's possible from Gracklen on Draxxt."

"Yes. You're right." Reginald flung himself onto the tawny leather couch and put up his feet on the sixties-style coffee table. "You think?"

"What are you going to do now, Reg?"

"I still have a job. A damn good job. I'm CEO at TopStrategy Marketing. I think I'll hire the old managers back. I think I'll take a demotion. I think I'll see if my old boss can come back. He was good to me. And I was a one-shot wonder, after all. I can't do better than the Millennial Goggles."

"Want a job?" Timothie grinned.

"My old job back," Reginald said. He grunted. "Are you offering me a shot at the salon business? I'd have to leave corporate management. I'll think about it. I've always wanted a business partner. And a salon of my own. Come to think, it would be better than middle management in a rather inauspicious marketing career."

"Don't be greedy now. I didn't say anything about a partnership."

"You want a silent partner?"

"We can meet with my lawyers in the morning. I'll draw up the papers."

"I love you, Timothie."

"Love you, too, Reg."

The lights went out.

About the Author

Kenna McKinnon is a Canadian freelance writer, author of *SpaceHive* (2012), and *Bigfoot Boy: Lost on Earth*, as well as *Benjamin and Rumblechum, The Insanity Machine*; *Blood Sister*; *Short Circuit and Other Geek Stories*; *DISCOVERY: A Collection of Poetry*, *Den of Dark Angels*, and *Engaging the Dragon*. Her most memorable years were spent at the University of Alberta, where she graduated with a degree in Anthropology. Kenna is a member of the Writers' Guild of Alberta and a professional member of the Canadian Authors Association. She has three wonderful children and three grandsons. Her hobbies include fitness, health, drawing, reading, walking, music, cooking and baking for friends.

Author's blog: http://KennaMcKinnonAuthor.com
Facebook: https://www.facebook.com/KennaMcKinnonAuthor
Twitter: http://www.twitter.com/KennaMcKinnon
Goodreads: http://www.goodreads.com/author/dashboard
LinkedIn: http://www.linkedin.com/in/kennamckinnon
Amazon Author Page:
https://www.amazon.com/s/ref=nb_sb_noss_1?url=search-alias%3Dstripbooks&field-keywords=kenna+mckinnon

Lightning Source UK Ltd.
Milton Keynes UK
UKHW041034161120
373486UK00001B/145

9 781715 776176